From the very beginning, he'd sensed something was different.

Jack had been deeply affected by the way Abbie spoke, by the genuine inflection of her laugh. He'd heard a depth of perception that he'd never ever heard from Natalie.

Yet he'd shunned all the indicators, hoping that the physical reaction he'd experienced was simply that of a mature man and woman coming to terms with all they'd shared as teenagers. Now he wasn't so sure. About anything.

"I enjoyed the time we spent together, Jack," Abbie said contritely. "I'm only sorry I'm not the person you thought."

But as he drove off, he was left with the mind-bending realization that he'd just made a horrendous mistake.

He'd been chasing the wrong sister.

Dear Reader,

As spring turns to summer, make Silhouette Romance the perfect companion for those lazy days and sultry nights! Fans of our LOVING THE BOSS series won't want to miss *The Marriage Merger* by exciting author Vivian Leiber. A pretend engagement between friends goes awry when their white lies lead to a *real* white wedding!

Take one biological-clock-ticking twin posing as a new mom and one daddy determined to gain custody of his newborn son, and you've got the unsuspecting partners in *The Baby Arrangement,* Moyra Tarling's tender BUNDLES OF JOY title. You've asked for more TWINS ON THE DOORSTEP, Stella Bagwell's charming author-led miniseries, so this month we give you *Millionaire on Her Doorstep,* an emotional story of two wounded souls who find love in the most unexpected way...and in the most unexpected place.

Can a bachelor bent on never marrying and a single mom with a bustling brood of four become a *Fairy-Tale Family?* Find out in Pat Montana's delightful new novel. Next, a handsome doctor's case of mistaken identity leads to *The Triplet's Wedding Wish* in this heartwarming tale by DeAnna Talcott. And a young widow finds the home—and family—she's always wanted when she strikes a deal with a *Nevada Cowboy Dad,* this month's FAMILY MATTERS offering from Dorsey Kelley.

Enjoy this month's fantastic selections, and make sure to return each and every month to Silhouette Romance!

Mary-Theresa Hussey

Mary-Theresa Hussey
Senior Editor, Silhouette Romance

Please address questions and book requests to:
Silhouette Reader Service
U.S.: 3010 Walden Ave., P.O. Box 1325, Buffalo, NY 14269
Canadian: P.O. Box 609, Fort Erie, Ont. L2A 5X3

THE TRIPLET'S
WEDDING WISH

DeAnna Talcott

Silhouette
R O M A N C E™
Published by Silhouette Books
America's Publisher of Contemporary Romance

SILHOUETTE BOOKS

ISBN 0-373-19370-X

THE TRIPLET'S WEDDING WISH

This edition published by arrangement with Harlequin Books S.A.

Look us up on-line at: http://www.romance.net

Printed in U.S.A.

Books by DeAnna Talcott

Silhouette Romance

The Cowboy and the Christmas Tree #1125
The Bachelor and the Bassinet #1189
To Wed Again? #1206
The Triplet's Wedding Wish #1370

DeANNA TALCOTT

lives in Michigan where her three school-age children fill
her outside-writing hours with swimming, diving, baseball, basketball, wrestling, 4-H and Scouting activities.
Her husband has a career in law enforcement, and she
fondly dubs him a "professional volunteer" during his
off hours. Together, they enjoy making pilgrimages to
her childhood home near Lincoln, Nebraska, where
DeAnna grew up riding horses and attending a one-room
schoolhouse. As graduates of the University of Nebraska
at Lincoln, both she and her husband remain avid
Big Red fans.

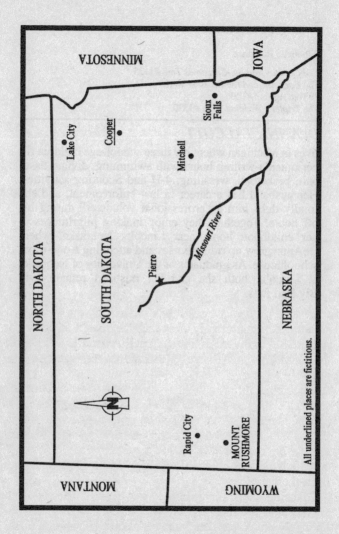

All underlined places are fictitious.

Chapter One

Abigail Worth zipped into Woody's, grateful the drugstore was typically dark and cool and quiet. Maybe no one would notice her new designer haircut—the one she'd foolishly driven all the way into Sioux Falls for this morning.

Unable to stop herself, she paused at the cosmetics counter, self-consciously checking the length in the oval mirror. She cringed, then rearranged around her ear what the hairdresser must have considered the salvageable leftovers.

Amazing. It was impossible to believe what one pair of scissors had done. She'd asked for something new and sporty, and the hairdresser had cheerily hacked off fifteen inches of length, spiked the top, left her shoulders naked and the back of her neck cold and exposed. Huh. Her father could have done better with the rusted pair of sheep shears from the barn.

Glancing away, she grimaced and yanked her collar up another notch to hide her lily-white neck. Pivoting, she deliberately slunk past the bubble packs of hairbrushes and combs, hoping to go unnoticed.

But that was impossible. A person couldn't get by with much of anything in a small town like Cooper. Nothing. Not even a bad haircut.

Good grief, she'd never live this down.

She paused at the display of gift baskets containing bubble bath and shower gel and scented soaps. Picking up the smallest, she counted the others, thinking that it was a whole lot harder to change her image rather than start a business.

Ahh. Vanilla Musk. Now *that* was a comforting fragrance. She was glad she'd chosen it. It reminded her of her two favorite things: homemade cookies and potpourri.

Then, by chance, over the basket rim, she glimpsed him.

All six foot two of him. Her mouth slid slightly off center as she took in the same dark hair, the same blunt-cut chin and jaw. The pair of dimples that pitted his cheeks and bracketed his mouth. The slash of brows over his eyes.

Jack Conroy. Heartthrob, humanitarian and hell-raiser extraordinaire.

He was leaning against the pharmacist's window and talking to the man behind it, not really looking at her but quizzically eyeing the basket in her hand. His elbow was propped next to the ballpoint pen chained to the counter. One hip rode higher than the other, and with his ankles crossed, it looked like he'd been there awhile.

He'd been there awhile? Jack Conroy? Back in Cooper?

If she could backpedal, she'd do it in an instant. She didn't want to be caught looking like this—not fiddling with her hair and trying to wheedle another half inch from the roots.

Why, she knew Jack. If he recognized her, he'd say something clever. And the last thing she wanted was to be caught looking like the prize pet from a sheepshearing contest—one totally incapable of bleating back even one witty retort.

But, drat it all, her mind went blank. Just like always!

For as long as she could remember, she'd look up at him and her mind would pull the vanishing act—as if the man had somehow pulled the plug on all rational thought.

Well, it wouldn't happen today, she vowed. She wasn't some ditsy, gaga-eyed teenager any longer. She was a capable woman who intended to fashion an independent life for herself.

Yet she froze the moment their gazes collided, smashing into one another full force.

The penetrating look he shot her made her forget all about the promise she'd just made. She forgot about her hair. She forgot about her clothes and how uncomfortable she felt in anything other than jeans. She forgot about how her life paled in comparison with her sister Natalie's.

A giddiness, a euphoria, spun through her at the same time her knees turned to mush.

The slightly off-center grin she remembered, this time triggered by recognition, slid onto his face.

Jack Conroy.

And, believe it or not, he actually remembered her.

The boy with the bedroom eyes and the irrepressible smile.

In high school he'd fallen for her triplet sister, Natalie, and she'd stoically weathered their on-again, off-again relationship, pretending it didn't matter.

Jack inclined his head, cutting off the pharmacist with a "Catch you later."

His intense gaze, as if it was holding her hostage, never once drifted from hers. He moved toward her, skirting a mother and son and an end-cap display of doctor-recommended insoles. While she stood rooted to the wide plank flooring, he picked up momentum, sprinting past the old glass candy counter.

When he was within two feet of her—and with his dimpled smile widening—he threw back his head and laughed.

She didn't know if he was amused by her pitiful haircut or genuinely pleased to see her.

"You look great," he said.

"I...thanks," she breathed, unable to stop her right hand from finger combing through the new length at her nape.

But even as she struggled to make that first impression right, perfect, the spontaneity of the moment—of coming face-to-face with Jack after all these years—dazzled her. They stared at each other, and seconds ticked away as the backdrop of floor-to-ceiling shelving, of prescription bottles and over-the-counter remedies evaporated into one rosy-colored hue. The phrase from a popular country tune, the one she'd heard on the truck radio this morning, went zinging through her head: *Color my world, little country girl.* For that was precisely how bumping into Jack made her feel—as if traditional country and up-and-coming cosmopolitan were facing off.

"You look better than great," he teased.

"Jack..." Abbie glanced away, suddenly uncomfortable that Jack was no longer a hometown boy. He'd obviously outgrown Cooper. Now he wore designer aftershave and Izod sport shirts, and he purportedly had a slew of degrees decorating the walls of his doctor's office.

"What? Not even a welcome-home kiss?"

The suggestion sent a shiver of surprise up Abbie's spine. But Jack merely grinned, then threw his arms around her and swept her off her feet.

Abbie gasped, and the basket ended up crushed between them. Everything went Tilt-A-Whirl crazy as he swung her around. She squealed, winding her arms around his neck and letting her legs dangle as he squeezed her middle tight up against him.

"Jack!" she protested, leaning back. But she took him all in, seeing how much he'd changed, seeing if he was all she remembered. His skin was coarser, his beard heavier. She noted the hint of a receding hairline near his temples and the tiny laugh lines around his eyes. The details complemented each other, creating a more mature, more confident man.

She glanced back at his eyes, unnerved to realize his baby blues were giving her the once-over, too. From skimming a look over the top of her schizo hairdo to glimpsing down inside the button front of her scrunched-up shirt.

She stiffened, painfully aware her breasts were squashed right up there against his own heaving chest.

He never seemed to notice.

"My, but don't you look good," he whispered, squeezing her tighter as he spun on his heels. "Ten years. And you haven't gained an ounce. And that awesome smile—it's still the same."

Abbie's throat closed right up, cutting off any cutesy reply. She pointedly scanned the narrow aisle, focusing in on all the expensive baubles they were going to smash. "Jack! Watch it! We're going to break something!"

"So? This time around, I can afford the damages."

Perhaps he could, but given the tremulous beat of her heart, Abbie knew she couldn't. Not where Jack Conroy was concerned. Clinging to him, she lifted both shoulders. "Maybe you can, but not me. I…well, I…"

He slowed, then stopped. Putting her down gently and using her warning as an excuse to pull her even tighter and closer against him, he looked down and into her face. "That better?" he whispered, the implications definitely sexual.

She couldn't breathe. She couldn't answer. Sensations—his scent, the texture of his knit shirt beneath her fingertips, even the way his chin hovered an intimate inch above her brow—overwhelmed her. But what was worse was that his mischievous gaze refused to waver.

He chuckled. As if he knew exactly what he was doing to her—and as if he'd gotten the intended response.

Suddenly, an ominous premonition mushroomed inside her. "Jack? Wait a minute. Jack, do you know who—"

He shook his head before sliding a forefinger over her lips to effectively shush her. His assessing glance darted from her lashes to her brows and forehead, to the razored cut at her temples. He frowned at her ear, quizzically tapping one new dangly earring.

"I—I got them pierced a couple of years ago."

He nodded, the corners of his mouth twitching. "I see that." But Jack dropped his gaze to her mouth, to the rose-tinted shade the stylist at the recent makeover guaranteed as kissproof, and Abbie's heart lurched.

Two breathtaking seconds passed. Then a third. She thought she'd die if he didn't say something soon.

"My birthday," she said breathlessly. "I got them pierced for my birthday."

The corner of his lips lifted. "I don't remember you liked making small talk before," he said, his voice husky as his wrists slipped beneath her elbows. His forearms warmed the undersides of her breasts and his palms met at the center of her back.

Before she could stop him, his fingers inched up her spine.

"Jack? What're you—"

"Shh, honey…let me do the talking…and, this time, just let me say…I've waited ten years to do this right."

His lips swooped over her mouth and claimed it.

The kiss was borderline tense, as if he was holding himself in check. As if he truly had a decade of self-restraint and need to account for.

Yet that was the last logical thought Abbie had before she slipped away and lost herself to the feel, to the impressions that were solely Jack Conroy. Her fingers discovered the label stitched to the back of his shirt. His cheek was damp, moist, as if he'd recently shaved. He smelled of a comforting combination of soap and sport scent.

She tried to pull back, to remind herself they were in Woody's in the middle of the day. But she just couldn't manage it. It was as if she was drowning in everything that made Jack Conroy unique.

He tilted his head to one side as he kissed her, and she felt his lips firm into a smile when she responded. Joy and heady enthusiasm were all rolled up into one. Physically they swayed; emotionally they were headed straight down the garden path of instinctive desire.

Then the basket crunched between them. The cellophane crinkled and bottles of bath salts clinked against each other. The sounds were muffled by her breasts, his chest. But the vibrations were hard, insistent.

It served as the wake-up call they both needed.

Abbie straightened her shoulders but still pressed herself tightly against Jack to save the basket. At least that's what she told herself when she first heard the murmurs in the background.

But she lost ground when a second wave of pleasure hit her, when his tongue probed, leaving only dizzying sensations.

When the giggling began, Abbie was barely conscious of it.

Jack reluctantly pulled away, his lips still brushing hers as he sighed. His forehead dropped against hers. "Looks like we drew quite a crowd," he whispered. "I imagine that was the biggest show in Cooper all week."

"I—I, um...Jack..."

Still locked in his arms, Abbie twisted her head out from under his chin. She looked around his shoulder to those who'd gathered in a semicircle around them, to those who gaped and giggled and nudged each other.

Mrs. Wilcox stared over her bifocals. Mr. Bitterman dropped his package of corn plasters and didn't seem the least bit interested in picking them back up. The Osten twins rolled their eyes and made gagging noises. Balding

Mr. Cheney muttered something to his arthritic wife about, by damn, wishing *he* was five years younger.

Abbie winced, then said aloud to anyone who would listen, "I—I'm sorry. It's, um, been so long, and—"

The pharmacist guffawed.

Abbie turned beet red.

It didn't help when Jack chuckled, too.

"Come on. Let's get out of here before you make any more apologies." He turned her toward the front of the store and pushed her forward. "Right now, you're all mine. And I'm not sharing."

The fascinated cashier at the front window quit craning over the counter and tried to look busy when they moved toward her. But the girl failed miserably. Abbie, who moved woodenly, was mortified.

"Only this," Jack said, shoving the basket of bubble bath at the teenager. He reached in his back pocket for his wallet. "This is a lady who likes, and expects, the finer things in life."

"This?" The disbelieving girl accepted it. But her eyes nailed Abbie for confirmation.

Abbie struggled over a refusal. "Jack, no. Please. You don't have to do that. Because I was only looking. See, I—"

"I *want* to do it for you," he emphasized, his arm dropping possessively into place at her waist. "Let me." He gave her another quick peck on her temple against her wispy new hairdo. Abbie had no idea a kiss could feel that good, sound that good. "We'll take it," he repeated to the cashier.

Abbie struggled to come to her senses. "But...Jack, you—you don't understand that I—I..." Abbie was so befuddled with all the strange new sensations flooding her that she could only stare as the cashier wrapped the basket into two squares of tissue paper. She didn't have the strength to explain that the purchase was a mistake.

"Your change, sir."

"Thanks." He slipped the coins and bills into his pocket without even looking at it. Without taking his eyes off Abbie.

That did something to her, the way he looked at her. It was so reminiscent of the past. She wanted to bask in the moment at the same time as she wanted to stop it.

But those big, beautiful blue eyes.

The quick-witted retorts that had always danced behind them. The shrewd blue intensity.

She couldn't help herself. She let it happen.

He handed her the basket of toiletries and took her elbow. "Enjoy."

She stared at the package, not quite comprehending what to do with it. "Thank you," she said automatically, feeling like a ninny.

"A welcome-home gift. From me to you." He guided her, leading with his shoulder to push open the heavy, old-fashioned wood and beveled-glass door.

As they stood on the sidewalk, Abbie suddenly realized how little had changed since they were teenagers. The heat, the dust. The same false-fronted buildings, the same town square with the antique threshing machine chained to a concrete slab. The tiny, white wooden pavilion where, for posterity, they had scratched their initials into the varnish on the picnic tables.

Everything was the same except—when she was standing beside Jack—everything felt different.

"But, Jack," she said carefully, "I am home. You're the one who—"

He turned her toward him, his hand firm on her elbow as he paused long enough to torment her with his dazzling smile. It vaguely occurred to her a man this handsome shouldn't be allowed to roam the streets of South Dakota.

"Guess what? I've got a surprise for you, babe...."

The door finally whooshed shut behind them.

"You—you do?" she ventured.

"You bet."

From her peripheral vision, Abbie saw the park bench in front of Woody's and ached to collapse into it. She had the strangest premonition she'd need to be sitting down for this one. "Yes? Go ahead."

"I *am* home. At least temporarily. I've volunteered to fill in for Doc Winston until he finds someone to take over his practice. My mind should be on the job, but you're the one I've been thinking about, Nat. You're the one I want to celebrate these next few months with."

Chapter Two

Abbie stared at him. Natalie? He thought she was Natalie? "But—but I—"

"I know. I know it's a shock. Everybody figured I'd be in Omaha forever. But," he said, grinning, "when Doc Winston needed someone to fill in for him, I jumped at the opportunity."

Abbie shifted uncomfortably, uttering the only rational thought that skittered through her mind. "You actually wanted to come back to Cooper?"

"Of course. I've missed it."

He winked at her, and she remembered it as the same teasing gesture that had always nicked a corner of her heart.

How was she going to tell him? How?

It would be a letdown. The entire burst of emotion, the kiss, it would all be a letdown. It would be an embarrassment. For both of them. No matter what happened, they'd never be the same, or even feel the same again. They'd probably never be able to look at each other again.

"Hey! Let's do lunch! You and me. How about it?" The

compelling blue color of his eyes nailed her. "Ever reminisce about taco pizzas and bubble-gum ice cream?"

Abbie stalled, the reminder making her go into a cold, apprehensive sweat. He and Natalie had eaten themselves sick on taco pizzas. "Not—not a whole lot, no."

"How about we share them again? For old times' sake?"

She looked away, absently smashing the top of the Woody's bag. Maybe if she could get out of here without him ever knowing, without him ever finding out, then maybe she could save him the embarrassment. She knew she could save herself the hurt. "Jack, I'd honestly love to, but—"

"No buts. You can't disappoint me. I've been looking forward to this for too long."

"Jack. Listen. I'm—I'm not really the same person any more."

"Good! Because neither am I. Hey, come here." He casually tossed an arm around her shoulders, steering her toward the corner. "I want to show you something. You're gonna love it."

"What?"

"I want to show you how I've moved up in the world." Nudging her forward to the curb, he paused above the diagonal parking lines, near the hood of a persimmon-colored convertible. "I finally traded in my economy car and did something outrageous. You proud of me? You always complained I was too conservative."

"A convertible? Oh, Jack…it's beautiful."

"Not practical, but hey, it makes a statement. A whole lot different than that old Rambler I used to drive, huh?"

"A whole lot. And if anyone deserves it, you do."

He chuckled. "I swear the only advantage the Rambler had over this was those crazy reclining seats. Remember how bad we thought we were, kissing on the horizontal? Remember Miller's Pond and…"

Abbie blanched, never hearing the rest. Miller's Pond was the local lovers' lane. She'd never been there.

She quickly stepped down off the curb and out from under his arm to trail her fingertips over the custom striping. She leaned over the passenger door, feigning interest in the dusty black leather seats and wondering how she was going to remove herself from this insanity. "South Dakota will be merciless on this interior. You'll probably have to trade this in on something more practical."

"Forget that. I'll suffer." He took the curb in one giant step, meeting her on the other side of the car and digging in his pocket for his keys. "Come on," he said, opening the door. "Today we celebrate. Today we set this town on its ear."

"Jack, no, listen—"

"Forget it, babe. After lunch, you can start making excuses and spouting the serious stuff about how you have your eye on some off-the-wall entrepreneurial scheme. You can gloat over your own unconventional success story and apprise me of your lifetime goals. But all that waits until after lunch, okay? You owe me that much." He slid in and winked, then leaned across the seats to throw open the door. "Okay?" he repeated, patting the passenger seat.

Abbie stared at the spot Jack indicated. The spot next to him, for a thigh-to-thigh ride in his sporty little car.

Temptation grappled with logic—and Abbie, who had consciously chosen to change her life, took a split second to decide.

"All right," she agreed, sliding in and scrunching the basket of bath salts onto her lap. "All right, this time I'll do something impulsive. I refuse to think about how I'm going to live to regret it."

He grinned, and somehow his hand ended up on her kneecap. "Damn. I like the sound of that, darlin'." A current of electricity from his words, from his touch, shot through her. "Not only does it sound dangerous," he went on, "but it also sounds like a challenge. And you *know* how much I like challenges."

She blinked at him. His response was definitely sexual.

How had she ever tripped his wires?

Forget the fact they were identical—Natalie had been the only one able to do that before. Surely he'd be able to see, to feel, the differences.

Swallowing back her trepidation, she watched, mesmerized, as he slid the key in the ignition and rolled it over. The engine purred, and an unsettling thrum coiled up through her thighs, through her middle.

He put it in reverse before he reached over and squeezed the back of her hand, the one still clutching the bag of bath salts. "I'm telling you, you're better than ever, Nat. You make a man damn glad he waited."

This was crazy.

He had no idea. No idea at all.

Jack leaned back against the bench seat as he pushed away the black-bottomed pizza pan. "That was disappointing. Definitely not what I remember." He wadded up a thin paper napkin and tossed it over the crusts. "Funny how old age changes you."

"It's been ten years, Jack. Think we should pass on the bubble-gum ice cream, too?" She leaned closer, putting both elbows on the table. "I think we've both outgrown that."

He grinned, appreciating the intimate lift in her voice and the way she tilted her head when she spoke.

She was amazing. Simply amazing.

To him, the past ten years had only enhanced the way she moved, the way she talked. In South Dakota lingo, he'd say she'd gentled down some. In medical terms, he'd say she'd finally gotten a grip on the obsessive-compulsive behavior that had always driven her. Maybe college had refocused her need to be in the middle of the action, to take charge of the party.

Still, everything about Natalie Worth was remarkably quirky and inviting. She'd toned down the makeup and fired up the style. Her eyes were a tad more mysterious than he remembered, and that did something to him. He loved the sloe color she'd deftly stroked over the lid and slanted up at each corner, and the way her brows lifted every time he said something funny.

Her lips were fuller, her smile more sensitive. The kiss she'd pasted him with in Woody's had been extraordinary.

No doubt about it. *This* Natalie was definitely better.

"Come out and see the renovations I'm making on Gramps's place," he impulsively invited, suddenly reluctant to see the luncheon end. "It's sat empty for six months because no one in the family could decide whether we should put it on the market or keep it. But since everybody agreed it needed a face-lift, I volunteered for the job. I'm thinking about making the kitchen ultramodern." He waited for her reaction, expecting her to fast-forward into a dozen animated suggestions.

But she frowned, her lips crumpling. "Ultramodern? Jack! It's a turn-of-the-century house! It should be elegant country. With oak cabinets and a claw-footed table and—"

"A what?" He stared at her, puzzled by far more than her vehemence.

"A claw-footed table. You know, the kind with brass on the toes and—"

"I know, I know." His hand seesawed between them. "But if I remember rightly, you were the one who raved about sleek contemporary."

The recollection seemed to surprise her. She shrugged, obviously not knowing what to say. "That doesn't mean I don't appreciate things that fit well together. Chrome and glass just wouldn't make it in Gramps Conroy's place."

"Nat, this doesn't sound like you. Not at all. You always

knew what you wanted—and it was never country." He watched her mouth open, then carefully close. "But hey, it doesn't matter *what* you wanted. Come on out and see for yourself."

"I shouldn't. Really." She pulled back her silk cuff, rolling over her wrist to glimpse the time. The lunch hour had ended long ago and the waitress was shooting them dirty looks and cleaning up around them.

"But you want to," he wheedled, ignoring the waitress. "You know you do."

"Of course I do. I've wanted to see inside that old house for forever. It's like a mansion sitting out there on that rise. Like something out of a movie. Ever since I was little, I've wondered what it would be like to live in it, to—"

"You never told me that."

"I—I didn't?" She shifted, lifting her Coke glass and looking somewhat surprised there was nothing left but ice cubes and watered-down pop. "I probably thought it would sound like I was inviting myself in."

"Come on, Nat. You never had any compunction about inviting yourself anywhere. When we were juniors in high school, you wangled an invitation to every party and then you twisted my arm to take you."

"I never twisted your arm," she muttered, staring down into the dregs of her Coke glass.

"Excuse me?"

She looked away, absently flicking the edge of the paper place mat with her fingernail. "Um, I said I don't know. I shouldn't. It's probably not a good idea. It's late and—"

"This is your chance. A private tour." He watched her, gauging her reaction before imprinting her indecisive expression on his mind.

This was a new vulnerable quality he'd never seen before. It changed the old feelings he had for Nat. It also aroused more intense ones.

"Oh, all right," she said finally. "I refuse to ruin your 'welcome home' day, no matter what it does to my life."

The wonderful smile that had stirred a passion in him as a teenager eased onto her lips. Only this time she gave it to him differently, softer side out.

Natalie had evolved into a kinder, gentler soul. Yet she still possessed her stunning good looks, looks that had matured and refined her.

"Kind of you," he said slowly, considering, as he put all the new bits and pieces of her together. "Especially since you never had much patience for indulging me."

"Jack, I'm not indulging you. I'm curious. That's all."

"Great. So we'll put your curiosity to rest."

She let him guide her all the way to the car.

That puzzled him, too, only because it wasn't like Natalie. Not at all. Natalie was one to sprint ahead. She was one to take charge.

But, in true form, he had to admit she carried the conversation the entire two miles to Gramps's place. She pointed out changes in the countryside: who was living in the brand-new development on the outskirts of Cooper, who had left. She told him when the Owens' barn had burned down and how the McClintock boy had forged his daddy's signature to a dozen Co-Op checks and wound up in jail.

But she was conspicuously silent about herself—and her family.

Even though it bothered him, and he vaguely wondered why, he rolled into the driveway feeling positively euphoric. He'd wanted Natalie Worth's undivided attention ever since she'd taken that dare and run off with his jeans when he was sixteen, buck naked and swimming in the creek. Her defiance and determination, though sometimes grating, had always amused him.

After what he'd been through these past few months, he'd relish a diversion.

"I love it out here," he said, braking as they approached

the sprawling white clapboard house. He angled the car to the southwest corner of the wraparound porch. "Look up there." She followed the direction of his gaze to the peaked roof, the trim and cupolas. "I'm painting the whole thing cream. Then I'm doing the gingerbread trim in teal and green, the window frames in sunset and flame. What do you think?"

"What do I think?" She laughed, lifting both brows. "I think it's outrageous."

"No. Really."

"I think your grandpa would insist that's way too fancy for a ranch house." He lifted an apologetic shoulder. "But—" she gave him a sideways glance "—if you're asking me, I love it."

That was the only confirmation he needed. "Wait'll you see the rest of what I've got in mind," he said, stepping out of the car.

Like everyone else in Sanborn County, he'd left the front door unlocked. He opened it and ushered her inside. Drop cloths trailed up the curved staircase and hung over the banisters.

"Sorry," he said, kicking one aside to reveal hardwood floors, "I'm stripping wallpaper tonight."

She stepped around the paintbrushes and buckets, her eyes darting over the faded grapevine pattern. The dusty-colored leaves and vines gave the foyer a jungle effect.

"Busy, huh?"

Abigail stared overhead to the second-story tin ceiling, where an antique fixture hung from a long, dark chain. "It is sort of overpowering."

"Sort of? Nat, I'd expect you to make some nasty crack about the tastes of my forefathers."

The remark made her chuckle, her shoulders shuddering as she poked her head into the adjacent dining room. "My heavens. Did you really have sit-down dinners here?"

"Every Sunday."

She shook her head, taking it all in. "How did you ever come to our house? Our old table was so scarred and beat-up and...and *used*. This is extravagant."

The sheer curtains at the bay window billowed as a slight breeze moved the dry, dusty scent of the unused room.

"Maybe that's why I preferred your place. It was lived in."

She glided into the cavernous room, past the tarnished candelabrum on the buffet, past the linen-covered walnut table, to pause at the window seat. It was upholstered in button-tufted red velvet, long faded, the welting threadbare. "This is gorgeous," she remarked. "Just this one little corner puts my imagination in overdrive."

He smiled, rocking back on his heel to lean against the door frame. "What do you see?" he asked, aware that for one brief, fleeting moment she looked genuinely serene, content.

"Eyelet pillows. Plants and baskets of magazines. A reading nook right here in your very own dining room. Something cozy and warm and..." She trailed off, looking away as if she'd said too much, revealed too much.

Sinking a knee onto the window seat, she pulled aside the curtains to look out on the porch to the neglected flower beds. A moment of silence hung suspended uncomfortably between them. He wasn't sure why.

"Maybe I should hire you to do the consulting work on the decorating?"

Her eyes were riveted to the rolling expanse of the landscape. "Sorry. I've already got a job."

"Doing what? You never said. I knew you were back in town. I ran into Collins. He said—"

"Yes, and that newspaper job's behind me now." But she said it too quickly before hesitating and briefly pursing her lips. "What do I do? You know me, Jack. It's always retail. I'm always trying to sell myself." Letting the curtains fall, she rose and turned back to him, a too bright smile on her face. "Hey, I'm ready for the rest of the tour. Make it good, and give me all the lurid details. I heard your aunt Aggie once chased a preacher off with a shotgun. That true?"

He grinned, stoically refusing to divulge family secrets as he led her up the stairs and through each of the five bedrooms. Then he showed her the way down the back stairs to the main floor. The kitchen, she agreed, was a Depression-era nightmare.

"I often wonder how Gram put a meal together in here," he said, skimming a forefinger over the top of the refrigerator to measure the dust. "The whole thing has to be gutted."

"Still..." She pivoted in the middle of the room, her eyes drifting from the ceiling to the wainscoting, then to the traffic pattern worn into the vinyl. "There's a feeling, an aura, that lifts you up the moment you walk in. I like that. It feels comfortable and well-worn."

"I hope you're not talking all-American and apple pie, Nat."

She shot him a quizzical look.

"It just doesn't fit, not you."

"I'm telling you, Jack. I've changed."

"So I've noticed. Well, we all have, but—" spreading out his hand, he indicated the white enameled cabinetry, all mismatched, and the single tin sink with double taps "—I mean, come on."

She laughed. "You're spoiled from all the modern conveniences, from all the technology the doctor in you has come to expect. It isn't like that out here."

"Hey! I know that."

"I'm warning you, Jack, you're going to suffer culture shock. You'll be so glad to get back to Omaha, people will think your shirttail's on fire when you leave."

"Forget it. Coming back will be all I remember and more."

Her expression became strangely somber. "Nothing's ever the same as you remember," she said slowly.

His eyes slid over her again, from the top of her knock-out hairdo down to the buttons on her fuchsia blouse. "Some things are even better. Like memories and wine...they age well."

The undercurrent of suggestion hummed between them—until she suddenly, unexpectedly, turned her back on him. At the door, she pulled aside the panel curtain and stared into the yard.

"How are you going to get all this work done?" she asked, her gaze straying to the machine shed that needed paint and the barn that needed shingles. Weeds had grown knee-high in the rusted wire fencing and thistles had taken over the pasture. "It's not just the house. It's the outbuildings and yard, too. And did you forget Doc Winston still makes house calls? That he's the only one around who's on call twenty-four hours a day and that everyone in the county takes advantage of it?"

"I haven't forgotten."

"Jack. You could have—" she looked over her shoulder at him, obviously exasperated "—you could have done better. You should have stayed in Omaha where people pay you what you're worth. Out here..." She trailed off, her hand lifting.

For a moment, neither of them spoke.

"You still don't think I have enough ambition, is that it?"

"I never said that."

"You didn't have to. Only Natalie Worth would be gutsy enough to point out that a man who stoops to be a country doctor compromises his talents."

"That's not what I meant." She hesitated, biting her lower lip. "Look, Jack, you could end up very disappointed by what you find here."

He stared at her, wondering precisely what she alluded

to. "I didn't come back looking for anything, Nat. But I have gotten pretty weary of working in ER," he said finally. The pitch of his voice dropped, and he couldn't stop himself from saying the rest. He wondered if she'd think less of him for admitting why he'd come back. If it would make him any less of a man in her eyes. He knew her attitude. He knew the scathing way she looked at people who couldn't cut it. "It was either get out or burn out. I decided the choice was going to be mine."

"Every job can be a grind. That doesn't mean—"

"No. This was different. This changed me. I started wondering what I was doing there, why I was trying to save people that really didn't care. The drunk drivers. The overdoses. The battered women. Sometimes I thought I was just a stopgap measure. I didn't…Nat?…sometimes I didn't feel like I was making a difference."

She blanched visibly, and he wanted to kick himself for being too candid. It was all too soon and he instinctively knew it. She wasn't prepared to share his gut feelings. Not yet.

"Jack, I understand your frustration. But…but, maybe you're telling this to the wrong person."

"I don't think so. We were always honest with each other."

She paled, her eyes becoming starkly luminous, nearly tormented. The curtain dropped back into place. "Jack, I don't think you really want to tell me this. And I need to go home. It's late, and…"

He stared at her. The good times, the fun of the afternoon forgotten? All because he'd shared some personal information?

No, she hadn't changed. Natalie probably never would.

She'd never wanted to become too close. Didn't have it in her to share personal stuff. She'd always protected herself. Just like in high school, she'd always made a point of reminding him everything they shared was only for fun.

But when he came back, he'd told himself that was all he needed.

"Sure," he said shortly. "I'll take you home."

They walked to the car in silence, he slightly ahead of her, focusing on every clump of watergrass pockmarking the lawn and trying like hell to remind himself of all the work he had ahead of him. When was he going to wise up? Natalie Worth had never been in his future. Never had been, never would be. But why the heck did her image always grate on his mind? It always taunted him as if all the potential was there and only had to be keyed in.

He made a show of yanking open the door for her, and when she flinched, he felt like a heel.

But instead of getting in, she paused, staring sightlessly at the interior. Overhead, the wings of a dozen Canadian geese plied the head winds. The air was sticky hot for September, yet there was an ominous suggestion of change to it. Her eyes shuttered closed, and she looked like she wanted to say something.

"Yes?"

"Jack, I should be honest with you."

"Okay."

He watched her snag a deep breath and briefly hold it. "You didn't need to buy me that basket in Woody's."

"What? Excuse me?" The sudden shift in the conversation to some insignificant gesture that had happened hours before confused him.

"You didn't need to buy me that basket," she repeated, scooping the package from the back seat and pulling it from the bag and tissue paper. With her palm on the iridescent cellophane, she turned the basket bottom side up. "I made it. It's a custom thing. I do orders and baskets on spec. Giftware. I needed something of my own, and..."

Jack didn't hear the rest. He read the stickered bottom, then went numb as a hot feeling radiated from the center of his chest. *A Tisket, A Tasket, Specialty Gifts by Abigail Worth.*

"I didn't know how to tell you. I was so happy to see you. Truly. But it never occurred to me you'd assume I was—"

"Natalie," he finished for her, his voice dry, flat.

"Yes. I'm sorry."

"You let me believe…intentionally believe…" He bit back the words, unable to finish the rest.

"Not intentionally, no."

"Like hell."

"Jack, it's been so many years. And the three of us, we're all so different now. I didn't even realize at first what you were thinking. Not until you called me by Nat's name, and then…" She apologetically lifted both shoulders. "Well, by then I didn't know how to stop it."

He felt a fury, an anguish, rise in him that he never imagined possible. His mouth dropped into a hard, thin line. They weren't teenagers anymore. The time for playing games was long gone. What the hell did Abbie think she was doing anyway? This wasn't like her. Not at all. Abbie was the one who was kind and sensitive, the one who always put other people first. "Cute. I imagine Nat'll get a big bang out of this one," he seethed.

"No! She's not like that. And I'm not. You know that. I won't ever tell her, Jack, not if you don't want me to."

He jammed his hand into his pants pocket, searching for his car keys. He wanted her out of here. Now. "Get in. I'll take you back."

"Jack, wait. I said I'm sorry. I…" She dropped a hand on his arm.

He stared at it, feeling as if he'd been scorched. The look made her carefully, slowly, remove her hand. After she did, he wondered inanely if some leftover adolescent hormones were rushing the spot, paralyzing it and wreaking havoc with his internal balance.

Abbie, innocent and unaware of how she'd affected him, straightened and began again. "It only got worse after I realized you thought Natalie was home again, that she was back in Cooper looking for a new job. I'm sorry, Jack, but she's found a new life in Rapid City. She's got a boyfriend she's head over heels in love with, and…"

He jerked the car keys free, saying nothing.

"You've every reason to be furious with me," she whispered. "I'm so sorry. I am. Everything just happened so fast. You thought I was someone I wasn't. And I thought I'd be letting you down if I didn't go along with it. So, as stupid as it sounds, I let it happen. I know I shouldn't have. I…"

He walked around to the other side of the car and got in.

Abbie, because she had no choice, did the same.

He put the key in the ignition, but before he could turn the engine over, she stopped him.

"If it's any consolation," she said softly, "you should know this basket thing was Natalie's idea. She once made the observation a person could sell anything packaged in a basket. I just put her idea into motion. In a way, it was natural for you to be attracted to it. It was a link, a connection. Maybe your subconscious picked up on it."

"My subconscious," he said flatly, "didn't pick up on a thing."

But, in truth, that was an outright lie. From the very beginning he'd sensed something was different. He'd been deeply affected by the way Abbie spoke, by the genuine inflection of her laugh. He heard a depth of perception, of appreciation, for the everyday things he'd never, ever heard from Natalie.

Yet he'd shunned all the indicators, hoping merely that the physical reaction he'd experienced in Woody's was simply that of a mature man and woman coming to terms with all they'd shared as teenagers.

Now he wasn't so sure. About anything.

"I enjoyed the lunch and the time we spent together, Jack," she said contritely. "I'm only sorry I'm not the person you thought."

"You've got no reason to be sorry," he said gruffly, throwing the car in gear. "Forget it. I jumped to the wrong conclusions, that's all."

But as he drove off, he was left with the mind-bending realization that he'd made a horrendous mistake. He'd spent his youth chasing the wrong sister.

Chapter Three

Abbie stared straight ahead into Schmidt's back pasture, conscious of the precious little time she had left with Jack. She felt numb. Stupid. Jack jounced over the potholes at the end of the driveway, then floored the accelerator, making her gaze stray to the dash.

The needle jumped from ten to sixty-five in the same amount of time it took the car speakers to belt out the chorus of Patsy Cline's, "I Fall to Pieces."

The passionate ebb and flow of the music were disturbing.

The lyrics were gut-wrenchingly honest.

She winced inwardly, feeling guilty and wishing she could tell Jack the honest-to-God's truth about why she had pretended to be Natalie. If only she could face him and tell him what she'd been thinking. If only she could tell him what she felt, what was in her heart. If only—

Jack snapped off the country oldies station with a decisive flick of his wrist.

Abbie blanched.

He hated her. She knew it.

For some moments, the hum of the wide, steel-belted tires echoed their mounting discomfort with each other. Abbie shivered and bit her lower lip, not knowing where to look. Not at the floor mats. Not at the console where Jack's palm was draped over the gearshift. Not at the telephone poles that went whizzing by in one big blur.

What she wanted was to look at Jack. To see how angry he was. To see if his chin was set and his eyes were glazed. But she couldn't bring herself to sneak so much as a peek— because she didn't want to know how much of a mess she'd made of their friendship.

She finally stared at the basket of toiletries in her lap. Stupid, stupid, stupid. She had so painstakingly labored over the silly thing. For what? Iridescent curling ribbons. Artfully crushed tissue. Soaps and gels and powders and bath salts. The whole thing mocked her.

She felt like the biggest nincompoop ever to walk the face of the earth.

Still, it blew her mind how Jack had so easily mistaken her for Nat. Aside from their physical resemblance, which had admittedly grown over the past years, Nat had been famous for a dollop of fire and a dose of dry humor. No doubt about it, with a full head of steam Natalie was a beauty.

She was, quite regrettably, unlike Abbie.

After their mother walked out on them when they were eight, they'd spent their youth battling through a parent-child relationship. Later, Abbie had mother-henned Nat through all four years of high school, often admonishing her with the *R* words: respect, reputation and reason.

Nat had merely laughed and chided her to get a life. But Abbie could still hear their quarrels, could still see her own wagging finger. The strange thing was, as sisters they loved each other deeply. They simply never understood each other.

How could Jack have mistaken her for Natalie? How? It was like comparing fire and ice.

Now that Jack knew the truth, he obviously realized it, too. Considering the way he hugged the door panel, it didn't take much brain work to figure out whom he considered the icicle.

She sighed, painfully aware the haircut and makeover hadn't made much of a dent in the image she'd created for herself. Everyone assumed she was the humdrum sister, the one who stayed home and helped with the ranch, volunteered at the library and didn't know how to tell so much as a knock-knock joke.

The one who hadn't been kissed.

Not until four hours ago.

In the cosmetic aisle of Woody's.

By mistake.

Her lips burned, remembering. She pressed the back of her hand over her mouth in an effort to lock up all the wonderful sensations Jack had awakened in her lonely body. She'd never known a man could make a woman feel that way, oblivious to everything but his touch.

And Jack, she ruefully admitted, had a very powerful touch.

She pressed harder, wanting to imprint the wonderful feelings, wanting to savor them for as long as she possibly could. Most likely, it would be all she'd ever share with Jack.

Suddenly, her eyes pricked and the corners grew damp. She squeezed her eyelids tightly, painfully shut, half-worried her new mascara would run.

God, she didn't want to cry. He'd think she was a ninny.

"Ab...?"

"I..." She cleared her throat, her knuckles brushing her nose. She realized the gesture must make her look as shamed as a prizefighter who'd lost the first round. "Um, I'm sorry. You must think I'm a terrible person."

"I don't."

She refused to believe that. Those were the words of a doctor who'd taken more than his fair share of psychology classes. "Right."

"I'm angry with you, though."

"You've every right to be. I should have stopped the whole thing instead of letting it get out of hand." She turned her head away, unable to bear seeing his expression when she told him the truth. "But the reason I did that was because…because I…" She stopped abruptly.

She couldn't manage it. She couldn't.

A hot, dry wind rushed the car, whipping her hair and the sleeves of her blouse. She couldn't seem to draw an ounce of it into her lungs. Her chest ached, and her head throbbed. She couldn't look at him, so she concentrated on beating back the pain. She stared at the sagging barbwire fence, the thistles needing to be chopped in the ditch.

Anything. Anything but Jack Conroy.

She detected an imperceptible drop in speed and knew his foot had lifted from the accelerator. They were a mile outside of Cooper.

So precious little time. Especially when a woman as uncertain as Abbie wanted to explain herself and resolve things.

"It can't be that difficult," he said smoothly. "Just tell me why. And we'll go from there."

"I…" She lifted her shoulders, but the words wouldn't come.

"We still could have done the same things. The lunch. A drive in the car. A tour of the house."

But it wouldn't have been the same, Abbie thought miserably. Not with your preconceived idea of me and who you think I am. Not with the kiss. Not with those few moments of intimacy.

"Why, Abbie? Why ruin my homecoming with a lie?"

"I didn't mean to ruin it!"

Two seconds spun into oblivion.

"Then?"

"Look. You just thought I was someone I wasn't. And you seemed so genuinely happy that I hated to disappoint you." The accusation rolled off the tip of her tongue so quickly, it surprised even her. "You would've been, you know."

"Forget that. I would've enjoyed seeing you, too."

"Don't tease."

"I'm not," he protested. "Call me crazy, but I prefer knowing whom I'm talking to. I'd rather have known it was the real you."

"Jack. Listen…" They were looking at each other then, face-to-face, as the car slowed to a crawl.

For one special moment, she memorized every detail. The way the wind had tossed his hair, the way his mouth parted and his eyes narrowed. The intense, almost perplexed look hovering in his blue eyes.

She'd walk over hot coals before she'd look him in the eye and tell him the truth. The truth was that she'd had a crush on him since ninth grade, when he'd grinned and winked at her and included her in a harmless prank a bunch of kids had planned for the science teacher. She couldn't very well tell him he'd thrilled her that long-ago afternoon. She couldn't tell him that ever since she'd wanted to be adored by him.

He'd classify her as a borderline spinster and eccentric to boot.

"You don't know the real me," she said softly, gently, unaware her voice had dropped to a whisper. Then she did something she'd always longed to do. She dropped her hand, her palm covering his wrist, the pads of her fingers brushing his knuckles. The gesture, though slightly awkward, sparked with familiarity. "You don't know me, Jack. That's the thing, and that's the reason why. The afternoon wouldn't have been the same."

"And why not?"

"Because if you had known I was Abbie, you'd have asked me all the same polite questions other people do. How is my dad, how are my sisters. You'd have mentioned the weather." She carefully withdrew her hand, indicating he should drop her off next to the dusty truck still parked on the diagonal in front of Woody's. He couldn't miss it, not with Worth Shorthorns stenciled on the driver's side.

"Abbie, that's lame. Absolutely lame. We could've talked about..." He drifted off, feigning concentration on turning in front of the oncoming traffic. "Oh, hell, I don't know what we could've talked about! I admit it—I can't think of a damn thing!"

In spite of herself, the corners of her mouth lifted. "See?"

"Ab! That's not fair." His knuckles went white as he frowned, grasping the steering wheel. "Okay. Here. We could've talked politics. Or global economy. Or movies...or...or I could've asked you about some of the kids we went to school with. Who stayed, who left, who got married. Who has kids. Hey—" he lifted an eyebrow "—that enough for you?"

She thoughtfully, slowly, shook her head. "No. You forgot something."

"What?" He made the turn.

"Me. You could've asked about *me*."

She felt like she'd blindsided him when his mouth dropped.

"But—but," he stammered, "that goes without saying, I mean, that you and me, we never—never really—"

"I know. It's no reflection on you, Jack. But don't you see? The afternoon was so spontaneous, I didn't want to spoil it when you learned the truth. You think you need to talk to me differently somehow. And, the truth is, you don't."

Something flickered in his eyes. She wasn't sure what.

But she had the uncanny feeling it would somehow alter what little they had left between them.

She regretted that.

It would have been nice to be able to walk away and say they were better friends than they'd been before. It would have been nice to say that at least they had one memory, crazy as it was, to share.

He pulled into the adjacent parking spot, and she pulled the latch on the door handle and was out of the car the moment he slowed to a stop.

"Here." She reached over, thrusting the basket at him. "I'll tell Nat I ran into you, and we'll leave it at that."

She had already turned her back on him when, "Abbie! Wait!"

"Yes?"

"Will you look at me? Please. Please?"

She reluctantly turned on the ball of her foot. It took every bit of resolve to lift her downcast eyes from the side molding to meet his steady gaze. "What?"

"Let's make a deal."

"And that is…?"

"We both made a mistake. So I won't tell anyone about this if you won't. Okay?"

"You don't want anyone to know?"

"No. Let's keep this little mix-up between us."

Without knowing it, he'd driven a spike into her heart. She felt the fantasy shudder, then wither and die a slow, painful death. "Sure. Okay. Today never happened."

"It only happened between you and me," he prompted.

"Whatever you say, Jack." She looked away, over her shoulder to the truck, trying unsuccessfully to bury the humiliation that was rising like bile in her belly. She felt sick, physically sick. "Look. I've got to go."

Climbing in the truck, she turned the key in the ignition and pumped the accelerator extra hard, hoping she'd kick the bejeebers out of the muffler that was on its last leg anyway. She wanted to drown out the thrum of his classy little convertible, her mushrooming pain and every crazy notion she'd ever had about Jack Conroy. But because she couldn't quite manage all three, she threw the truck into reverse and, without looking in her rearview mirror, headed out of town as if her tailpipe was on fire.

He'd made it clear he didn't want anyone to know he'd spent the afternoon with Abigail Worth.

Well, she'd show him. She swore she would.

She wasn't the same person he remembered, and though it might take some doing, intuition told her she'd soon have the opportunity to prove it to him. She just hoped he was ready for the transformation.

Jack had only one destination in mind, and after the fiasco with Abbie, he felt driven to get there. In less than ten minutes, he'd lose himself at the local hangout, Cooper's infamous watering hole, The Redd Rooster. He hadn't hung one on since med school, but right now he needed to get rip-roaring drunk.

At least his timing was significantly better than it had been with Abbie—Happy Hour was about to commence. In his mind's eye, he could see the beer mugs, like little tin soldiers, squarely lined up in front of him. He'd knock them back as if he was doing battle.

My God. He'd *kissed* Abigail Worth.

He couldn't believe it.

As far as he could recollect, nobody, but nobody, got within arm's length of Abigail.

But he'd done it.

Gone right up there, big as you please, and plastered her with a kiss that would have made a mewling kitten out of a lesser man. It was shameful, that's what it was. Part of him felt like a heel. An honorable man didn't treat a nice girl like Abigail that way.

But the part that got under his skin, bothering him most, was that she'd kissed him right back. Right there in Woody's, in front of everybody. As if it didn't matter one whit. Her face didn't go red-hot and she didn't look embarrassed, just thrilled to death to see him. Then he'd gone and swung her around looking like he was pretty darn familiar with her and had done it a thousand times before.

If word got around…

His eyes fluttered closed. Talk about gossip, speculation and a sullied reputation. Of course, he didn't know whose reputation he should be more concerned with—his or Abbie's. He knew everyone would have their eye on him. He was the new doctor in town; doctors were expected to maintain a modicum of respectability, of reasonable behavior.

They didn't go kissing women in Woody's, and they certainly didn't go off on benders, either.

But he *had* to get the taste of her out of his mouth. It was driving him nuts. He needed to saturate his senses, numb them. Right now, he couldn't quit thinking about the way she tasted, the way she felt. He'd never forget how she'd pressed up against him. So soft and curvy in all the right places, so firm and willowy in the rest.

Crumb. What had gotten into him?

Maybe this coming back to Cooper hadn't been such a great idea after all. To begin with, he didn't even like anything stronger than iced tea. He only had a beer if it was a hundred degrees in the shade and someone pressed one into his hand. But worse than that, he'd never taken advantage of a woman in his whole life. He liked to think he had some scruples.

Sure, he'd intended to get together with Nat. A little intimate exploration with her would have been pleasurable, even par for the course. Her behavior was notably outrageous.

But Abbie? He envisioned her, pristinely done up in gold and white, wearing a banner across her chest proclaiming Nice Girl Next Door. Everyone thought she was the sweetest, most innocent thing. All the guys he knew assumed Mother Nature hadn't equipped her with one passionate bone in her body. They figured she was so naive a sexual thought had never once gone flitting through her head.

Oh, brother. Had Mother Nature ever pulled one over on them.

He couldn't believe it. Everybody had ribbed him for years about Nat being the hot number. Man, the truth of the matter was that she couldn't hold a candle to Abbie.

Part of him felt like he'd just stumbled upon a well-kept secret, and now he was faced with figuring out precisely what to do with it.

Good God. He *needed* a drink. He needed to get his fuzzy thinking straightened out. What was going on? Had he lost it? Had the stress pushed him over the edge?

Abigail Worth?

And him?

Impossible. Absolutely, totally, irrevocably impossible.

Nobody kissed Abigail and felt their knees buckle. Nobody kissed Abigail and felt some earth-shattering quake tear up their insides.

Nobody. Not even him.

His reaction had to be based on the fact he *assumed* it was Nat. That was it. It was the only logical explanation. Abbie wasn't his type. She was sweet and kind and out-and-out bland.

Bland was something he tolerated in his diet, not in his love life.

He wheeled into The Redd Rooster, then slammed on the brakes so hard the car fishtailed on the gravel. Dust billowed over the trunk, putting a powdery film over the back seat. Abbie's words, and the honeyed tone of her voice, tumbled through his head uninvited.

South Dakota will be merciless on this interior.

Beer, he thought, stumbling blindly from the car. Beer, with a whiskey chaser.

The dimly lit Redd Rooster was a welcome change from the blistering late-afternoon sun. Jack squinted into the darkness. He wasn't looking for familiar faces, just familiar things. The strand of Christmas lights hanging over the mirror behind the bar. The deeply scarred wide plank flooring that always looked thirsty for varnish.

He headed straight to a battered bar stool, vaguely aware of the beer signs. They were the same, though significantly more flyspecked. He ignored the patrons—a couple of old geezers arguing over cards, teenagers hanging out by the billiard table, the couple executing the familiar mating ritual next to the jukebox—and tossed his leg over the padded vinyl bar stool.

"Whatever you got on tap," he said to the bartender.

The man, with jowls oddly reminiscent of misshapen apples, glanced over the tops of his wire rims. "Not picky?"

"Nope. Not today."

Before the bartender could set two up in front of him, someone slapped his back. "I swear, Jack Conroy! The rumors must be true. So you're filling in for Doc."

Jack pasted the expected smile on his face and looked up, pleasantly surprised. "Will! Hey, good to see you." Their ensuing handclasp was warm, genuine.

"Yeah, someone said they saw you and a lady friend driving around town today."

"Yeah." Jack, reminded and prickling with guilt, glanced at the plastic bear draped over the Hamm's clock. Will was a former classmate; he was obligated to say something about Abbie. "Ran into one of the Worth triplets. Checked things out with her."

Will lifted both brows, making them disappear into the mop of curly blond hair hanging over his forehead. "What? Nat's back in town?" He threw back his head and roared. "Whoa. You don't waste time. You came into The Redd Rooster to crow about it, did you?"

Jack opened his mouth intending to clarify the matter. As he'd agreed with Abbie, they didn't need to broadcast the mix-up. Before he could reply, Will jabbed his shoulder.

"Private joke. Get it?" he prompted. "*Crow* about it."

"Yeah. Yeah." Jack tried to smile, but his honesty dissolved. He stared at the beer mug the bartender plopped down by his elbow, realizing this was going to be harder than he imagined. As shameful as it was, he changed the subject. "So, tell me about yourself. What're you doing?"

"Workin' for the county. Damn good job. Got lucky when a slot came open three years back on the road crew."

Jack nodded, throwing back eight or ten ounces of his first beer while Will kept up the one-sided conversation. Considering his bloodstream ran like pure springwater, it was only moments before a light buzz hit him. He added a dash of salt to what was left of the head, then polished it off.

"...and then, after that, I got married five years back. Girl from over near Madison."

"You don't say."

"Yep. Got four kids and a mobile home to show for it. Another on the way. Kid, that is. Reckon by next year, we're gonna have to get us a double wide."

Jack reached for the second beer and nodded to the bartender to keep 'em coming. After fortifying himself with a long swallow, he picked up the saltshaker.

"So what about you, Jack? Where you been since med school?"

"Omaha. Spent three years in ER. I learned how to put

folks back together, and when the pieces didn't fit, I learned how to make do.'' He watched the grains of salt drift to the bottom of his mug, stirring up dainty threads of effervescence.

''Amazing what they can do these days.''

''Isn't it just?'' He pushed the saltshaker back. And when the parts aren't available, he wanted to say, I learned to fall back on a few lame phrases of comfort for the grieving families. ''Yeah, you make a few miracles and muddle through the tragedies. On the worst days I used to figure it was a fifty-fifty crap shoot.'' Knowing his philosophy bordered on the maudlin, he forced a grin. ''Taking over Doc's general practice for a few months will be a snap.''

''I imagine with Mindy expecting and the cold and flu season setting in, you'll see her and the kids.''

''Provided you trust me with their welfare.''

''Everybody knows you, Jack. You're a person who does the right thing by everybody.''

One more stab of guilt pierced him as Abbie's face floated through his consciousness. Jack pushed the visage away, determined to talk about how bad the fishing had been this year, how the taxes for the new roads had jacked up the price of license plates and how, according to the *Farmer's Almanac,* they were in for a bad winter. Then he couldn't stand the small talk a moment longer.

''Look, good seeing you, Will, but I gotta go.'' He slid off the bar stool. ''You take care.'' He got two steps away before turning back. ''Say, I meant to correct you, but the conversation kind of got away from me.'' He paused, gauging his timing. ''It wasn't Nat I ran into, Will, but Abbie. She's a rare one, isn't she?''

''Abbie?''

''Yeah. Spent the whole afternoon trying to figure out what makes her tick. Doesn't it strike you as odd a woman as desirable as her still lives at home?''

"I..." Will's brow furrowed. "Abbie?"

"Yeah. Abbie Worth. You know what? I'll bet before I'm done here, I'll make sense of this thing yet."

He left, never seeing Will's poleaxed expression or the way his old friend shook his head, then picked up and threw back Jack's last, untouched beer.

Chapter Four

Jack turned the basket in his hands, marveling at the distinctive touches. Every detail was a testament to Abbie. So like her, to take a simple basket and create something special from it. He'd put it beside his bedside table last night and woken up looking at it.

He'd debated about calling her last night. He'd stared at the phone number on the bottom of her business card, and a pang of nostalgia hit him. It was the same number he remembered. He must have dialed it a thousand times.

The first calls he choked over. Later, he got smart and feigned extraordinary interest in homework assignments and bus schedules, talking with whichever triplet he was lucky enough to connect with. Eventually, when he praised Natalie's geometry expertise, she fell for his suggestion they study together.

The dozens of memorable calls after that, where he hung on Natalie's every word, were charged by her flip remarks. Nat's flirtatious demeanor never waned; loyalty was another matter.

The remainder of the calls had been lovers' quarrels. The

make-up, break-up stuff. The last time he'd dialed the
Worth number was on the eve of graduation. He'd tested
his maturity by swallowing his pride and wishing Nat a
happy, successful college experience. He hadn't spoken to
her since.

Strange. After ten years, he'd given a lot of thought to
giving Nat a call, hoping he'd come back to Cooper and
find her settled, changed. He'd never, ever expected to
come back and find out what the intervening years had done
to her sister.

He'd gone to bed last night thinking of Abbie. He'd
woken up this morning thinking of her. He couldn't put the
indecision out of his head.

He needed to see her again. See if she was all he'd imagined. Maybe his recent move had somehow undermined his
FDS—the response mechanism he'd fondly dubbed his
"female defense system."

Damn. Something had definitely gone haywire. If it was
actually attraction he felt for Abbie, he needed to overhaul
his wiring with a trip to the Caribbean and take in a hearty
dose of white sand beaches and string bikinis.

Up until yesterday he was absolutely certain he went for
sophisticated types. Types who knew the ropes when it
came to the dating scene. Types who tossed on designer
labels and read *Cosmopolitan* and *Glamour* while they endured hours-long waits to have their hair permed or their
nails done. Types who preferred glass and chrome rather
than border prints of blue ducks and pink hearts.

There were no two ways about it. He needed to test his
mettle by confronting the real thing: Abigail Worth.

At four minutes after ten, the sun had already inched up
in the sky and tossed off another brilliant day. Jack turned
into the Worth drive, confident he'd timed his visit accordingly. Abbie's father, he thought smugly, would be out in
the fields.

He'd get Abbie alone, reassure her they were still friends and tell her he didn't have any hard feelings about what happened yesterday. He'd forgive her; she'd forgive him for getting angry about it. Simple as that, and easy as pie.

He intentionally chose the front door because the back one had too many memories. He'd loitered on that doorstep too many summer nights, spurred to leave only when Bob Worth stomped on the ceiling, reminding Natalie to cut out the horseplay because it was well after midnight.

Once on the front porch, he drew a deep breath, knowing exactly what he'd do. He rapped on the screen door.

"Just a minute!"

There was scuffling behind the front door as if Abbie was dragging something away from it. But he was completely taken aback when she flung it open.

"Yes?"

"Ab...?" Despite a view distorted by the galvanized screen, his gaze trailed over the satiny pink thing clinging to her shoulders.

"Jack? Omigod! What're you doing here?"

"Well, I..." He knew she had to be unaware the scrap of pink froth had parted to expose her tank top. It dipped dangerously low at the hollow between her breasts. "Look. Can I come in? This is something I've got to see for myself...." He caught his mistake, corrected it. "Um, say for myself. *Say* for myself," he emphasized.

She hesitated. "Sure. Sorry. Come in." She flipped the latch. "You took me so by surprise, I forgot my manners. Don't know how we ended up standing with a door between us."

"Damned if I know, either," he muttered.

She innocently held open the screen, her forearm on the crossbar as she stood sideways. The pink thing slithered up her arm and over her elbow, the front of it parted, looking disheveled, inviting.

He figured he should look away from the lingerie barely

covering her chest but couldn't quite look her in the eye, either. He glanced over her shoulder to the safety of the worn room he remembered.

One glance and something inside him snapped. His eyes widened at the two pairs of panties draping a fluted lamp shade. Black and salmon pink. The black pair had satin-ribbon roses at the juncture of the off-center seam near the thighs. The pink pair boasted provocative lace cutouts. He moved toward them as if he was on autopilot, then tripped over a beat-up blue laundry basket.

Abbie grabbed his arm, pulling him back before putting him on his feet. "Here. Let me move that."

"I'm okay, I'm okay," he said. But, given what he saw, he was anything but okay. The room looked like some lingerie jungle at a cathouse. A gold lamé bustier was propped against the back cushion of the sofa, and a garter belt straggled over a pillow needlepointed with the message Home-made Pleasures Gladden The Heart.

He wobbled, wincing over the rush of heat trickling into his groin as Abbie kicked the laundry basket out of the way.

He glanced down and went weak.

A whole basket of undies. Rumpled silks and pouffy satin panties. A gossamer nightgown. A molded push-up bra in a wild leopard print.

"Sorry," he apologized lamely. "I caught you in the middle of laundry."

"Laun...?" She paused, suddenly taking in the room. "Oh. No. None of it's mine."

He couldn't stop himself. His eyes traveled over the flimsy little thing slipping and sliding over her shoulders.

"What? Oh, this? This?" Her shoulders shuddered before she yanked it off. The tank top, pulled taut, volunteered the second unnerving secret of the morning: Abbie wasn't wearing a bra.

The realization stunned Jack. He felt aroused.

"I was checking the size."

"Uh, yeah." He tried to clear his throat. "I see."

"For a gift basket," she clarified, her cheeks flaming as she folded the bed jacket over her arm. "For a bridal shower, actually. To make things lively. To have for...well, you know...fun."

"Fun?"

"At the shower. And...after, I suppose."

He chuckled.

"Well, you're the doctor," she said hotly. "You should know about hormones."

He leaned back on one hip, assessing her and thinking just how fascinating this entire scenario was. Abigail Worth, explaining hormones to him.

"Hormones were not my specialty. But go ahead, tell me. Tell me about hormones, Ab."

"Not your specialty, my foot!" She couldn't hold it in any longer. She gently punched his arm at the same time the smile reached her eyes. What a wonderfully refreshing reaction she offered. "Jack, you're awful! You are!" she said, laughing. "You're intentionally making this worse, and then I'll probably end up apologizing for it, too."

"Probably."

"Jack!"

He grinned, then decided to come clean. "Sorry. But I came here to be serious. And I can't do it. Not with all this distracting stuff lying around."

"Okay. Let's try the kitchen. All I've got in there is dirty dishes. We'll get a cup of coffee to sober you up and—"

"Can't. I've got an appointment at eleven."

"Oh. All right."

It disturbed him the way her face fell, as if he'd personally rejected her. "I stopped by to bring you this." He offered her the basket of toiletries she'd left in his car. "I thought maybe—"

"Of course," she said brusquely, her businesslike demeanor making her breasts lift beneath the tank. "I can refund your money or send the basket on to Nat. Whichever you'd prefer."

"I don't want the money, Abbie."

"Then I'm sure Nat—"

"Forget Nat. She'd never appreciate how special it is."

"I'm sure if she knew it was from you—"

"I don't think so. Besides, we don't give each other gifts anymore."

"But yesterday—"

"Yesterday was an impulsive gesture. I brought the basket over because it's for you. I saw the look on your face when you got a whiff of the perfume. I want you to have it."

Her brow wrinkled indecisively. "Jack…"

"Cooperate with me. I know you well enough to know you don't have a dozen bottles of this stuff on your shelf."

"Well, no, I don't. I was waiting until—"

"That's your problem, Ab," he said softly. "You're always waiting. Sometimes you have to take what you want." The expression on her face subtly changed and whatever it was he said he knew it registered.

"Another impulsive gesture?"

"Nope. Not at all. I bought this basket for the lady who knocked me for a loop in the drugstore yesterday." A second passed before he added, "That lady was you, Abbie."

She looked down, beyond the fringed hems of her jean shorts and her bare, wiggling toes. When she lifted her head again, her expression was troubled. "Jack, thank you, but you don't have to do this. I'd understand if you're still mad at me and—"

"I'm not. Of course, you never said you forgave me for the way I acted when I found out who you really were."

"I…never thought a thing about it."

"Sure you did. You thought a lot about it."

"Well, I'm not admitting I lost any sleep over it, but—"

"You, too?" he interrupted. Her mouth dropped. "Pity both of us lay awake last night," he said.

Abbie crossed her arms protectively over her middle, and for one insane moment, Jack felt like he knew exactly what she was debating over. How much to tell him. How much to share.

"I'm sorry. I felt…like I really blew it, Jack. Like here I had this chance to get to know you all over again, and I ended up trying to impress you, trying to be somebody else rather than myself."

"You're pretty impressive all on your own, Abbie."

"Don't be silly. What have I done but stay home and grown older? You've gone out and made all these things happen for yourself, for your patients and your practice."

He didn't acknowledge the compliment. "That's pretty self-deprecating. Even for you, Ab."

"Well, I'm not feeling sorry for myself, if that's what you think."

"I'm not."

"I just had obligations here. I chose to do them."

He nodded. He knew exactly what she meant though she wouldn't say it or take credit for it. The Worth family wouldn't have hung together if it hadn't been for Abbie and her spunk. When her mother up and ran off, leaving her husband with three little girls, it was Abbie who looked out for everyone. It was Abbie who took responsibility for putting routine back in their lives. Bob Worth was a helluva rancher and a remarkable father, but it was his daughter Abbie who had sacrificed herself to see the family through.

It wasn't until this precise moment that Jack ultimately realized the price she'd paid. He thought of all the years of fun he'd hoarded, all the experiences he'd relished. She'd had none of them.

For a mind-boggling moment, he saw her as she saw herself: she was getting older, and life was passing her by.

"Abbie? You ever had regrets about things you didn't

do?'' he asked suddenly. She didn't reply, only looked up cautiously at him from beneath lowered lashes. "I have," he went on. "I've regretted we didn't know each other very well in high school. But now, with me coming back, what do you say we get to know each other again?"

She stared at him, with eyes so hopeful it made his heart throb. He wanted to put his arms around her lonely little soul and say it was okay, that he understood. But he didn't dare. This woman was capable of doing strange things to him, things he didn't quite understand. Given the situation he'd recently come out of, it would be prudent to go slowly.

"How about if we put yesterday's fiasco behind us and get to know each other over dinner this Saturday night?"

"Dinner?" she ventured as if she hadn't heard him correctly.

"Unless you're busy Saturday."

"No…nothing special."

"Well, then, I guess it's a date." She gave him a feeble smile. "Someone told me The Badlands still serves a mean prime rib, and I hear the band isn't half-bad, either. Unless you know of a better place."

"No…"

"You don't want to go?"

"Jack, you don't have to do this. If you're trying to make things right, remember I'm the one who made a mess of them."

So that was it. She was giving him an out. If he was a wise man, he'd pounce on the opportunity and flee. He didn't need to complicate his life a second time. Yet gut instinct told him that Abbie, if anyone, could mend what was broken in him.

He turned on the charm and leaned closer. "Okay, I admit it. I've got an ulterior motive, Ab."

"You do? And that would be…?"

"I hate eating alone," he whispered, tilting his head

down close enough to brush against her new haircut. "Come on. It'll be fun."

As he waited for her answer, part of him wondered what he was bargaining for.

"If you're sure it isn't a make-up date."

He handed over the basket, feeling the pinch of electricity when their fingers met. "Even if it is, I figure we owe each other."

She grinned but didn't seem upset. Hugging the basket against her middle, a quick, awkward moment passed between them.

He backed toward the door, suddenly groping for words like a kid who was suddenly uncomfortable with the goal he'd set out to accomplish. "Saturday night, then, okay?"

"Yes. Great."

"I'll pick you up at seven?"

"I'll be ready."

"Well, okay." His back was against the screen door. He pushed it open and stepped onto the porch. "See you then. Don't, um, work too hard straightening all this stuff out." He waved his hand over the scattered lingerie. "It's better when it's all loose and kind of rumpled."

"You know that? For a certainty?"

He felt his mouth tightening as he chuckled. "I do. Trust me on this, Ab. I do."

He winked and jauntily trod down the front porch steps, turning to face her only when he rounded the car. He waved, secretly pleased she'd stepped out onto the porch, shouldering the screen door and holding it open as she waved back.

When he jumped in the car, he found himself humming the first song that popped into his head. *You are my sunshine, my only sunshine…*

"Ye-ess!" he said aloud when he wheeled onto the highway. He felt like a kid again. Rejuvenated. Better than he had in months. Years.

And it was all because of Abbie Worth.

Chapter Five

After Jack left, Abbie ecstatically replayed his visit. She thought of the way his eyes toyed with the lingerie she'd purchased for the shower. They'd practically popped out of his head when he saw the fancy pants she'd tossed on the lamp shade. And the pink bed jacket he'd caught her in? She felt all warm and fluttery just thinking about his reaction.

Amazing. To think that Jack Conroy had lost his composure and tripped over a laundry basket. The memory made her laugh out loud. She was still grinning when she singed the meringue on the lemon pie.

Her father, who was washing his hands at the kitchen sink, eyed the pie and asked what she had to be so confounded happy about.

"Well," she said, pulling the pot roast from the oven, "I had a visitor today. Jack Conroy."

"Nat's old boyfriend?" Bob Worth jerked the hand towel off the bar and worked it between his palms.

"Well...yes. Of course, they haven't seen each other for

years. Probably since graduation." She handed her father the meat platter, then turned back to the stove.

"What's Jack doing back here?"

"Taking over for Doc Winston. Until Doc gets his retirement in order and finds a replacement."

"So he came out to check on Nat, I suppose."

"Well, no. Actually—" Abbie stirred the gravy one last time and turned off the burner "—we ran into each other yesterday. He came to see me."

Her father, already seated, stopped digging into the mashed potatoes. "You didn't mention it."

"I had other things on my mind. Like that bridal shower." She handed her father the bowl of gravy before sitting down opposite him. "Jack's renovating the old Conroy place," she went on. "He took me out to see it."

Her father sat back, completely unaware he'd let the short-handled ladle slip back into the gravy. Abbie fished it out with her fork.

"Jack plans to get the house all finished and on the market while he's here. So anyway, I left a basket in his car and he stopped by to return it. He asked to take me out for dinner Saturday night."

Abbie surreptitiously glanced at her father. He was meticulously buttering a slice of bread, taking the margarine to the edge of the crust. Not a good sign.

"Dinner," he repeated.

"Just to catch up." Feeling her father's eyes shift to her, Abbie hacked the slab of roast into wafer-thin slices. "So. Wasn't that nice of him? To suggest getting together?"

"Abigail…"

"He looks the same. Only older. I recognized him right off."

Her father laid his knife aside and propped the bread against the edge of his plate. "Do you think this is wise?"

"What?" She feigned innocence, stabbing a bit of roast and lifting it in the direction of her mouth.

"Don't give me that. You know what. He dated your sister."

"So? It was years ago."

Her father glanced at her shrewdly before taking a moment to squash the gravy through the tines of his fork. "You better think this over, Abbie. Sometimes certain feelings don't change. No matter how many years have gone by."

"Daddy! He asked me. And I said yes. What was I supposed to do—ask if he still has feelings for Natalie? Even if he does, it doesn't matter. It's only one night."

Her father hesitated.

"Daddy, we're just friends."

"But you didn't have a boyfriend in high school, Abbie."

Abbie winced, shamed by the reminder. "So?"

"So I'm not sure you understand the feelings that stay with a teenage romance, that's all. Your mama and I—"

"Were high school sweethearts. I know," Abbie interrupted, cutting him off.

"Situations like this get sticky, Abbie."

"Daddy, we're just friends. Do you want me to ask Nat's permission or something?"

He paused, then chuckled. "Nah. Knowing Nat, she probably doesn't even remember him."

His reply, astute as it was, made Abbie smile. Yet she was left with the uncanny suspicion something over and above Jack Conroy was on her father's mind. He'd been moody lately. But then, it was harvest. It could be the crops; it could be the cattle. Experience told her to let it drift.

Yet her father's reminder did have one strange effect: Abbie couldn't blot Jack's face, paired with Natalie's, from her mind.

Doubts and insecurities poked holes in Abbie's anticipation of her first—and probably last—date with Jack. Yet each time another ugly thought reared its head, Abbie dismissed it. When she came close to calling Jack and backing out, she went shopping instead.

Her first purchase was a new dress. Electric blue broadcloth, with sexy round buttons running straight down the front from the neckline to the hem. She ripped the tags off the moment she walked in the door so, no matter what, she'd have to keep it. She ironed it that very afternoon and hung it on her closet door to remind herself she *was* going out to dinner—and maybe even dancing—with Jack Conroy.

She worried about everything they'd talk about—and some of the things they wouldn't. She rehearsed her story about Nat, determined to keep it casual.

Natalie's busy with her new job. We don't hear from her much, but she's happy as a lark with the new man in her life.

Happy as a lark? That was overdoing it. Nat was spontaneous, never happy as a lark.

She thought about what she'd say about her sister, Meredith. *Meredith's remarried her ex and lives the high life in Chicago.*

For three nights in a row, she tried on her new dress, stared at herself in the cheval glass and resolved to make Saturday night the best in her life. Then she silently repeated her affirmations, a technique Meredith once confided kept her on track in the business world. Abbie had joked that it was a bunch of hooey; now she longed to be proven wrong.

I deserve this.

I deserve to build a relationship with Jack.

I am in charge of my own happiness, my own destiny.

I am confident and competent and easy to talk to.

She said each of her personal affirmations ten times, thinking if anyone witnessed the bizarre spectacle of the brainwashing she was inflicting on herself, they'd guess she'd been to the loony bin and back.

But she refused to give up.

Then, on the last night before their dinner date, she looked in the mirror and had a revelation. The dress, without the right accessories, was lifeless, flat.

Abbie dove headlong into hysteria.

What was wrong with her? Had she missed out on the gene that guaranteed "style"?

Dull and plain. That's what Jack would think.

The image of him, restrained and silently suffering through a tedious dinner, flitted through her head. After it was all over, he'd limply shake her hand at the back door, then politely thank her for the pleasant evening.

The likelihood of how the date would end made her queasy.

She went to bed and tossed and turned, hugging one of the three worn-out teddy bears that she and her sisters had dragged around for years, and willed away her fears and insecurities.

God, she wished she had somebody to talk to. She wished she had someone to say it was okay to be twenty-nine years old and scared and lonely.

Abbie, without a word to her father, got up extra early on Saturday morning and headed out for the nearest mall, determined to find something that would make Jack sit up and take notice. Like an Amazonian warrior, she foraged through gold and silver, name brand and off brand. In the end, she bought three necklaces, four pairs of earrings, two bracelets, a new pair of shoes and a matching handbag. She came home exhausted but vindicated.

To justify the expense, she told herself she deserved it—and, this time, to her surprise, she said it automatically, without having to convince her mirrored reflection.

That evening, she was ready fifteen minutes early, minus

three necklaces, three pairs of earrings and a bracelet. She felt like a different person when she floated down the stairs.

"Well, well, well." Her father looked over the top of the paper to inspect the results. "Don't you look nice."

"Thanks." She couldn't stem the smile that crept onto her face and self-consciously turned the bracelet around her wrist. "You don't think I overdid it, do you?"

Her father laid the paper aside. "Nah. Just hope Jack appreciates what he's got here. I always said you were the pick of the litter. Your sisters knew it, too. That's why they each, in their own way, loved you best."

"Oh, Daddy…" Abbie suddenly choked up, knowing he was trying to prop her up if the evening turned out to be nothing short of dismal. "Daddy, you always know what to say. You do."

"Hey. Three girls gives a man lots of practice. Especially knowing when he should rein in."

She knew what he meant. He didn't approve of this. Not one little bit. But she was an adult, and it wasn't any of his business.

Abbie glanced at the front windows, hoping Jack would be early. There was nothing left to do. The house was spotless, smelled like chocolate cake—in case she needed a dessert—and the radio was seductively low, tuned to a mellow country station.

"Want me to leave the radio on?" her father asked.

"Would you? That would help."

Her father chuckled. "Abbie, the standard line is 'I'll leave the porch light on for you.' It's that, not the radio."

"Mmm, but then again, I'm not scared of the dark," she absently replied, her attention drifting to the windows again.

"Yes, and that's not why fathers leave the light on, either." He levered himself out of his favorite armchair and headed for the kitchen. "It's a reminder, honey, that a man expects his little girl to be treated right."

"You know Jack. You don't have to worry about him."

"Huh."

Abbie went to the window and pulled aside the drapes.

Her father poured himself a lemonade, then spent the next ten minutes rustling the paper and offering up small talk. It drove Abbie crazy.

Twenty more minutes passed. Jack was late.

"Says here the jury in Grand Forks is still out on those charges against that meatpacking company."

"Oh?" Abbie couldn't have cared less. Only one thing dominated her mind. Jack Conroy.

Where was he? How could he do this to her?

"They say the way the case went on and on just about ruined the company. Probably put a lot of folks out of a job."

"I suppose." Abbie wanted to scream; she didn't want to discuss Royal Fork Meatpackers.

"Been better off if they'd settled the strike."

"Probably."

If Jack stood her up, she'd be so humiliated she'd never be able to face her father again. She'd never be able to live down her humiliation or the foolishness of all her silly daydreams. She'd toss out the cheval glass. She'd never be able to look at it again without thinking of the affirmations she'd doggedly repeated.

Delusions, that's what they were. Delusions of grandeur.

Oh, right. Her walking on the arm of Jack Conroy. Holding his hand. Sharing his dinner, his life, his joys, his sorrows. His future.

Right. The only future he could offer her right now was a humiliation so deep it cut to the bone. Her only saving grace was that she'd told no one, no one but her father.

The whole thing made her so mad she wanted to spit and stomp her feet.

If Jack stood her up, she'd send him the bill for the dress, the jewelry, the shoes that were pinching her feet, and the handbag that was the right size to be sophisticated but not big enough to hold everything. She'd itemize the cost of her humiliation right down to the penny. She would. She swore it.

She should at least get minimum wage for the hours she'd been a slave to her worries. It was only fair. She should at least be able to tell him—

Her father lowered the paper, looking over the top of the front section. "Is that a car I hear?"

Abbie bolted off the couch and whirled to the front door, yanking it open. It never crossed her mind she should appear unruffled, unconcerned.

No one in South Dakota was fashionably late. No one. It was probably the neighbors saying they had a cow out, or Gus from down the road asking if he could borrow the mower he'd called about. It wouldn't be Jack.

But Abbie froze as Jack bounded up the steps.

"Sorry," he breathlessly apologized, one-handing the button on his sport coat before reaching for the handle on the screen door. "It's all my fault. I should have called."

"That's okay," she heard herself say in a honeyed voice that had somehow floated outside her body.

"These are for you."

Abbie eyed the thin package of green florist's paper. Her fingers went numb, and every rational thought fled as she accepted it. "A peace offering?"

"Not at all. The reason I'm late. Mrs. Dolan closed early. I promised her a free allergy shot Monday if she'd open up special."

"My. Being a doctor does have its perks."

"It does. Amazing bargaining power."

"For flowers."

"Flower. In the singular."

Abbie stripped the florist's paper away. A single long-stemmed red rose. Her bruised feelings and shattered hopes resurfaced when the waxy stem slid through her fingertips.

Jack winked at her, his dimples doing a number on his personal sex-appeal quotient. "American Beauty."

Innuendo hung heavily in the air.

"I…" Abbie, so taken aback, couldn't drag her eyes away from the perfect petals or the moisture still clinging to the leaves. "I better get a vase," she blurted. "I never thought you'd do this."

He chuckled, his eyes lighting approvingly on her hair, her clothes.

When she turned to go to the kitchen, he moved into the room, extending his hand. "Mr. Worth. Good to see you again, sir. No, please, don't get up. We won't stay. I hope I haven't botched the dinner reservations."

"The Badlands can usually come up with a table." But Bob Worth's gaze followed his daughter into the kitchen.

"I know. But…" Jack's eyes quizzically flitted to the kitchen doorway, "I requested a certain table and was hoping that—" he lifted a shoulder "—oh, you know, that we wouldn't have to sit next to the kitchen with the clatter and all that."

Bob Worth reluctantly rose, tossing the folded paper on the chair cushion as he picked up his empty lemonade glass. "I hear you're going to be in town awhile."

"A few months. Until Doc decides what he wants to do about his practice."

"Been saying for years he's going to quit and go fishing. Of course, nobody around here believes that."

"I think this time he may be serious. Provided his replacement is a comfortable fit for the community."

"So do I have to go over the old rules with you again, Jack? Curfews and all that?"

Jack grinned. "Not unless I have to have this one home before midnight, too."

"Nope. I reckon Boo'll know when she's had enough." Without thinking, Bob Worth had slipped into using Abbie's pet name. Abbie had once been the "Boo" in the

Peek-A-Boo T-shirts her mother had fashioned for her toddler triplets.

Abbie entered the room, wiping a speck of water off the bottom of the vase. "Thank you, Jack," she said, placing the vase on the dining-room table so the rose arched toward the front room.

"Better take a wrap, Abbie," her father advised, picking up the paper and folding it to put under his arm. "They say the temperature is supposed to drop."

Abbie turned to the closet, thinking she'd never seen her father as distracted by a newspaper as he'd been tonight. He hadn't even been polite to Jack. She pulled out her new red wool coat and dropped it over her arm.

"No. Wear it," Jack said, taking it from her to hold open. Abbie slid her arms into the sleeves, a shiver unexpectedly going through her as his knuckles, warm and purposeful, brushed her nape. "I've left the top down on the car. Maybe by the time we get to The Badlands we'll see stars."

I'm already seeing them, Abbie thought dizzily.

They said good-night to her father, who only nodded.

Outside, at dusk, the ranch was serene. In the north pasture, cattle lowed, and the scent of red clover sweetened the air.

When Jack held the car door open, Abbie felt like a queen. For one fleeting moment, she figured all the conditions were right for an out-of-body experience. For that must be what this was, this dreamy, self-absorbed state. This remarkable headiness.

Life was turning around.

How many times had she watched Nat jump in the car with Jack? How many times had she wished she'd been the lucky one he'd chosen?

She was living her dream. Right here. Right at this very moment.

He slipped in beside her, and she smiled at him shyly.

"I goofed," he said, automatically starting the car as he faced her. "Your father thought giving you a single rose was, for lack of a better word, cheap. I didn't win him over."

"No. He didn't think that."

"He did."

"Well..." Abbie refused to address her father's concerns. "Forget it. I didn't. You didn't have to bring anything at all."

Jack put the car in drive, casually tossing his arm over the back of her seat. "I want you to know I could have given you a whole bouquet of roses, Abbie."

"What? Why would you do that?"

"For having the gumption to go out with me tonight. I imagine you had a lot of second thoughts. But I thought about it and figured one was a whole lot sexier. And, for you, that just seemed right."

Chapter Six

Sexier? Abbie's mouth hung open. She was unable to fathom how easily the statement rolled off Jack's tongue. He saw her as sexy?

Holy moley. Those affirmations must be working.

She silently thanked Mer for the advice, then spent the next two hours blossoming into her newer, sexier self.

"Okay, okay." Jack, his elbows on the table, leaned closer, pushing aside the remnants of the caramel torte he'd insisted they share for dessert. "We've gone overboard with this reminiscing. I know more than I ever wanted to about how Meredith broke her arm in seventh grade. You say you're sworn to secrecy. But I can't see you covering for Mer."

"Hey. If Daddy found out, during haying season, that Mer broke her arm jumping off the principal's porch—to put a match to a bag of horse manure—he'd have grounded us for the summer. No way was I putting myself in isolation with my two sisters."

Jack chuckled, but Abbie experienced a fleeting premonition. She'd opened the door for him. Here was his opportunity to ask about Natalie. She braced herself, comfortable enough to spew out her carefully rehearsed reply.

But he never asked. Just pulled his napkin off his lap and tossed it over his dessert plate. "Dinner was terrific."

"It was. Thank you, Jack."

"The company was better."

"Thanks." Abbie mimicked his moves with the napkin, smiling shyly. She wondered if the evening, stellar as it was, was over.

"I like this getting-to-know you business."

"Me, too. It's the first time we really talked. Just you and me."

His mouth twitched, and his dimples popped into place, his eyes twinkling as they narrowed. "We talked with you in that bed jacket the other day. But, then, that was definitely a distraction. I probably said some pretty dumb things."

"As if, in your profession, you don't see bed jackets every other day."

"Abbie..."

"What?"

A flirtatious spark hummed through the air, charging it, electrifying it.

"The thing with bed jackets," he said huskily, "is that it depends on who's in them."

"Hey. It was only me," she protested.

"I know. And one bed jacket does a lot to change an image."

Abbie stared into his compelling blue eyes, uncertain and giddy, wondering if he was actually flirting with her.

"Dance?" He tilted his head in the direction of the couples who swayed on the dance floor.

The music was slow, sensual, with a pulsing beat. Fear and anticipation thrummed through Abbie. If she said yes, he'd put his arms around her and hold her. They'd move together, just the way she'd always imagined.

But what if she stepped on his feet? She'd end up apologizing all over the place for being clumsy, that's what.

What if he held her too closely, like a lover? Or, not close enough, like a sister?

One way or another, she could end up being disappointed.

Worse, he could end up feeling the same.

But she couldn't turn him down.

"I...yes. That would be lovely."

He stood, moving around the table to put his hand at the back of her chair.

Never had Jack seemed so tall, so commanding.

She rose slowly, vaguely aware of the saliva pooled beneath her tongue. She didn't know what to say. The flirtatious moment evaporated. Suddenly, things were serious, making Abbie apprehensive. Misgivings loomed, like the shadows lurking behind the band.

Abbie moved onto the dance floor as Jack's hand settled on the small of her back to guide her. His left shoulder shielded her right one in a protective, almost instinctive way.

After she turned to him and he took her into his arms, she found it amazing how easily they fit together. They only made it through one stanza before someone bumped into her, pushing her against his chest. His stance widened and her legs sluiced between his.

For Abbie, the moment was awkward, embarrassing, though her every nerve ending throbbed with awareness.

Jack appeared unaffected. At this angle, his chin and the high, wide plane of his cheek tantalized. She tried to imprint the sight on her memory.

"I don't think we've done this before," he whispered against her ear. His breath rippled through the wispy hairs at her temple. She shivered, smitten by the exquisite sensation.

"No. We haven't."

"We—" he drew her closer so they couldn't be overheard "—make this look effortless. But it isn't, is it?"

"I don't know exactly what you mean," Abbie said.

"We're both trying so hard, so aware we have all these years between us and no memories. In a way, it's like starting out all over again, isn't it?"

"There are advantages to that, Jack."

"There are." His hand moved lower, below her waist, his fingers splaying over her hip. "Of course, I like thinking about what little history we do share. Finding you in that bed jacket. Seeing you for the first time like that in Woody's."

She grinned right into his shirtfront, feeling safe for doing so. He couldn't see; he'd never know how close he'd come to echoing her private thoughts. He was holding her close, making her wonder if he couldn't feel her smile, couldn't feel it burning a happy little hole right there in the warm spot next to his heart.

"Abbie?"

"Yes?" The set was nearly over, and she wanted to savor it, the motion, the rocking side to side with Jack.

"I'd like to ask you out next weekend, but I can't." She imperceptibly stilled. "I'm on a short time frame with the house and I've already scheduled carpenters to fix the porch and reshingle. They'll stay till they're finished."

Abbie steeled herself. He was letting her down carefully, establishing the parameters of their relationship. What came first, what didn't.

"You have responsibilities, Jack. I know that."

Around them, people were leaving the dance floor. The melody had picked up, but the two of them still swayed to the same internal beat.

"The thing is, I'd like to do this again, but..." He sighed. "Like you said, I've got commitments, and a new job, and—"

"Jack, don't. We're here only to enjoy tonight."

"I'm painting every night next week. If you have nothing better to do, you could stop over and approve the color scheme."

She grinned, relief threading through her. "Wouldn't you rather I wore my painting clothes?"

He looked genuinely surprised. "Want to?"

"Mmm-hmm. I think that's how you make memories."

He laughed, nodding. "I'll bet you look good in painting clothes, too," he said, cranking up his moves to match the new, livelier beat.

They broke apart, dancing fast until they were both winded.

It was after two o'clock in the morning when they finally headed home. Abbie was exhilarated. They drove back to the ranch with the top down, the wind beating the cold into their cheeks. Their eyes teared and the tips of their ears went numb.

Jack picked out a CD and turned the volume as high as he could. The music rolled over the plains, forever lost to the frosty night. At first, Abbie laughed out loud, then started singing along, snapping her fingers and gyrating in her seat.

Jack grinned, watching her instead of the road.

She did her best Tina Turner impression.

He roared, then lifted his foot from the accelerator to pull over to the side. The car rolled to a stop in the desolation of the Dakota plains. "Hey, you," he teased. "You cold? Want the top up?"

The CD player still belted out heady vibrations.

"You just don't want me to embarrass you," she accused.

"Not at all. I don't want to freeze you out."

"Are you kidding? I love it. I love the way it feels."

His smile faded, and he stared at her. Long and slow and hard.

The mood subtly changed from buoyant to serious.

He put the car in park, his palm slipping from the steering wheel as he turned to face her. He threaded his fingers through her frazzled hair, smoothing it around her ear. "I don't want to kiss you at the back door, Abbie," he said, his thumb grazing her temple.

He leaned closer, and it never occurred to her to stop him. It never occurred to her to wonder why he couldn't wait for the traditional at-the-back-door good-night kiss. She only knew that she, too, wanted to taste him again.

His leather jacket pulled taut, *whishing* against the car seat. His breathing was low, the rhythm unnatural. "Come here," he whispered.

She moved slowly, accepting the fragile moment with clarity, with verve.

The hand that had been on the steering wheel moved in slow motion to her face. The feel of his palm was warm against her chin and a strange contrast to the way his icy fingers curved up along her jaw.

"You're cold," he whispered.

"You, too."

Abbie longed to flex her lips, to see if they were too stiff, too cracked and dry to create the sensation she craved. She never had the chance. His mouth covered hers, and all sensible thoughts scrambled out of her head.

They moved together, tasting, treating. He aroused something inside her that reached all the way down to culminate in curling eroticism. He encouraged her tongue to pass through the fleshy warmth of his mouth, to discover his teeth and frolic in the cavity where his tongue met hers.

She indulged.

Instinct took over where inexperience left off.

"Aw, Abbie," he breathed, pulling away for an instant to nuzzle her eyes, her nose, "how can you do this to me?"

"Jack?"

"You feel so good. So cold on the outside, so warm on

the inside. Damn, you're driving me crazy, woman.'' His head dipped for another experimental kiss.

Passion opened like a floodgate between them. Her coat gapped open and he reached inside. His hand splayed over her rib cage, but it was Abbie's breasts that tingled. Her nipples strained against the satin cups of her new hyacinth blue bra, and the undersides lifted away from the underwire. Her new matching panties suddenly felt damp, and everything inside felt full and flush and needy.

She wanted to be touched. She ached to be touched and loved and desired. Pent-up desire raced through her, making her body moldable, pliable and very, very receptive.

The weight of his chest as he settled against her was rock solid and warm. A ripple of muscle pulled his coat back and away. She reached inside. The pads of her fingers trod over his collarbone, then up to the expanse of striated muscle sculpting his shoulder.

He groaned, pulling his mouth away to drive kisses into the pulse points below her ear, in her neck. His tongue danced over her flesh, his lips intending to leave their mark.

Abbie heard herself whimper, sure she had never in her entire life experienced anything more heady, more compelling than this. She wanted Jack Conroy to teach her what being a woman was all about. She felt driven to pull him over her, to thrill to his touch, his words, his unmistakable need.

She physically ached for him to touch the deepest part of her.

It was she who pulled away long enough to reach for his hand and drag it over the fullness of her own breast. Jack arched as if some kind of painful ecstasy was shooting up his spine, paralyzing him. His breath ruptured from his lungs in short, explosive pants.

"Oh, Abbie, what're you doing to me?" He sounded wretched, torn. His head was all the way back, and the stubble on his chin grazed her brow as he pulled away to sink back against the driver's seat.

"I thought…I'm sorry…I—" Her startled words stopped abruptly midsentence.

"God, what're you doing? Apologizing?" He slumped, hooking his nape over the back of the seat. Then he laughed heartily, his eyes fixed on the heavens as if someone up there had played a mighty fine joke on him.

"What?" she prompted.

"Nothing."

"What?" When he didn't answer, Abbie poked him in the ribs. "What'd I do? Tell me."

He chuckled, his head swiveling on the seat. "What'd you do? Abbie. You just made one hell of an impression. And let me tell you, it's all a man can do to recover from it."

Abbie glanced around the clutter spilling from the living room into the dining room. Baskets, paper shred, twist ties, ribbon, cellophane and gift cards were jumbled all over the table. Seasonal items, plus a healthy supply of Christmas ornaments, claimed all four corners of the dining room. The rest—the baby stuff, the stuff for showers and weddings and birthdays—had somehow claimed every available space in the living room.

Her new business was vaguely reminiscent of *The Blob:* it kept inching into and devouring their living space. Yet, to Abbie, none of it mattered. None of it was threatening. Not one bit. She was rejuvenated and bursting with optimism. She wallowed in the chaos and loved every moment of it.

A year ago, she would have been scrambling to pick up and organize. A year ago, she would have struggled to balance her checkbook, worried fate had seen fit make her an old maid, destitute and impoverished. To console herself, she would have tied her hair back with a rubber band, indulged in a bowl of popcorn and suffered through a second-rate video on Saturday night.

Not anymore. Things had changed.

Her business was showing a substantial profit. Her love life was terrific.

She tossed another paper bag of artificial flowers into the far corner and grinned, thinking how she'd persuaded Jack to go with the border print in the dining room rather than settling for plain wheat-colored walls.

"What the...?" Her father stood back to survey the mess she'd made putting three dozen baskets together.

"Look." She tilted one up for his inspection. "Aren't they cute? The print shop ordered them. Everything a student needs in one tidy little package."

"Abigail. I've got some men from the Co-Op coming over."

"What!"

"I thought I told you. Didn't you check the calendar?"

"But it's always the first Monday. Always."

"We changed it, Boo. You going to be able to get this cleaned up and fix us a coffee cake, too?"

"Oh, Daddy..." She looked around, knowing she was doomed.

"Well, put all this junk in Meredith's room."

"I can't. It's full," she wailed. "I stocked up on mailing boxes and packing. Mr. Lohman wants me to package his honey for a Christmas mail order. You know the volume he has."

"Okay, Nat's room, then. It's smaller, but—"

"I can't." He stared at her. "Honey, Dad. Honey."

"Oh, for—"

"Well, I had to have the product. And he had these little crates made up special for the jars, and those take up space, and then—"

"Spare me, Abigail. But find something to do with this stuff. It's pushing us out of house and home."

She looked around, estimating how much she could squeeze into the coat closet. The rest she'd drag into her bedroom and the upstairs hall. The pity of it was that she'd never find anything again. It would take a whole morning to sort out, and with Christmas only eighty-nine days away, she couldn't afford to lose the time.

"This is out of control, Abigail. Call it old age, but I'd like to be able to find my La-Z-Boy and settle into it every once in a while."

She glanced at his chair. It was buried beneath five different colors of crushed tissue paper. "I'm sorry."

"Honey, I'm glad your business is doing so well, but—" he glared at the answering machine Abbie had recently installed "—I can't even use the phone anymore because you're always on it with orders, and the calendar's all cluttered up with dates and deals and deadlines. This isn't a home anymore. It's a business."

"The upside is it's showing a sizable profit."

"Abbie, I have other things on my mind. Profit is not one of them. I wanted to slow down a little. If we're battling all this stuff..." He left the rest unsaid.

"Okay. I'll see what I can do."

"You need a work space. We could fix up the toolshed, put in a space heater if you want."

Abbie shrugged, thinking of the dirt floor, the friendly little rodents who dashed in and out, scavenging for a few kernels of corn and nesting materials. They'd appreciate the paper shred, no doubt about that. "Give me a few days, okay?" But, because of something Jack had offhandedly mentioned, an idea took shape in the back of Abbie's mind. "I'll see what I can do about moving the mess elsewhere. You deserve that much, Daddy, I admit it."

Chapter Seven

"I got a six-month lease," Abbie announced happily as she waved the keys in front of Jack's nose. "To see how it goes."

"I don't believe it. You're some entrepreneur."

She smiled, looking up at the narrow, false-fronted building and thinking that it had character because it stood taller than those on either side of it. The broken upstairs window, the peeling paint and rusted screens translated into potential. "Isn't it perfect? A bay window, a back entrance, a showroom and an office. Even a kitchen and bath upstairs."

"I'm more impressed with the location." He swiveled, nodding his head toward his squat, nondescript doctor's office across the street.

Abbie's recent acquisition, formerly a Cooper law office, had been vacant for years. The glass insert on the front door was still etched with "Lenkowsi & Sons, Law Offices, Est. 1947." To complement the clapboard and fish-scale trim, she intended to decorate with antiques she'd salvage from the ranch.

She'd have a gift shop, a place to keep her mess and regular working hours to boot.

"I'll be open ten to four. And you can stop by for lunch," she said. "Between patients."

"You think we're going to have the time? You'll be fixing up this place. I'll be fixing up Gramps's."

Abbie, awash in enthusiasm, felt her new flirtatious streak kick in. "Jack? Are you saying the only things we have time for are our fixer-uppers?"

He grinned, his gaze dropping to caress her mouth, making the memory of their last passionate kiss hang heavily between them. "Not at all, Abbie. Not at all."

"Thank you. Because, if you think—"

He nudged her, shoulder to shoulder. "I was hoping you'd come over and help me paint the bathroom tomorrow night. I know it's not dinner and dancing, but hey, we do have a working relationship, don't we?"

"The bathroom?" Wrinkling her nose, she debated, estimating it was, at most, a two-hour job. Not nearly enough time to spend with Jack.

"I know. Close quarters, huh?"

Talk about the power of suggestion. It made her light-headed, reckless. "Mmm. Close enough to be a bump-and-grind operation."

"Bump and grind. Whoa-ho!" He threw his head back, laughing at the sky.

"It's so close we'll end up looking like we experimented with body paint or something."

"Abigail." He pulled back, feigning shock. "You surprise me."

"Oh, hush, Jack. You love every minute of it. You know you do."

"And where, exactly, did this body-paint thing come from?"

She toyed with the idea of letting him think it was all her imagination; she guessed he'd like that, and somehow she wanted to please him. But the truth, with Jack, held more appeal. "Remember that bed jacket?"

"That's not something a man would forget, Abbie."

"Well, you don't think lingerie was the only thing that went into the shower basket, do you? I had to scrounge up a few goodies. Body paint. Massage oils. That sort of thing."

Jack grinned. "God, I'd have loved to see you go through the checkout counter. Abigail Worth and body paint. What a devastating combination."

"*Edible* paint," she clarified.

"*Edible?* Really?"

"Mmm. So they say. There's probably not much food value in it." He snorted. "Flavored, too. I got orange, grape and piña colada. Whatever that is."

"Piña colada? Hah! I love it."

"So did the bride."

"No kidding." His lips twitched. "Funny thing you should mention it, Abbie. They've got piña colada on those little paint-chip charts. It was second choice for the bathroom walls, but I've got to admit there's something particularly intriguing about it now."

"Yeah. Very funny."

"I'm not kidding."

She ignored him, looking straight ahead to the front porch of her new building, where, next spring, she would arrange a rocker and hanging baskets of pink begonias.

"Okay. That settles it. Piña colada it is—but only because you've developed a kinship with it." There was a slight pause as he leaned closer, whispering seductively, "So. Wanna help?"

She couldn't resist; she smiled slowly, imagining both of them frolicking around in piña colada–spattered painting clothes and having the time of their lives.

"Dress casual," he advised as if reading her mind. "The painting party begins at six."

* * *

Abbie, with her new life zooming out of control, learned what it was to juggle, and she was proud to say she'd gotten the hang of it. But it amazed her how her life had veered from the straight and predictable to rolling down the fast lane with a business and a night life and a family.

She worked doubly hard at keeping her father in the center of her life. She intended to keep it as normal, as unaffected as possible for him. Even if she couldn't be around, she made certain his meals were ready, the house was clean and that he never lacked for a fresh shirt and jeans.

But it was beginning to be a trial, this old life–new life adventure. After penciling her father another note—the single serving of casserole would only need four minutes in the microwave—she told him not to wait up for her, that she'd be late.

She didn't tell him why because he'd tell her she was nuts to paint someone else's bathroom. Particularly Jack's.

Taking the steps two at a time, she ran into her bedroom to toss on a sweatshirt, which, by no stretch of the imagination, could be considered worn out enough to paint in. She paired it with her second-best pair of five-pocket jeans and compromised on her old tennis shoes. Jack never seemed too interested in much below the ankles anyway.

With the October weather still holding, seventy degrees and partly sunny, she commandeered the pickup, relishing the ten-minute ride to the Conroy place.

Jack was already there, his convertible, with the top still down, parked near the back porch steps.

"Hey! You're early!" He strode out the back door wearing bib overalls, no shirt and a happy smile. His bare shoulders were deeply tanned. A cheesy, thin painter's cap, on backward, covered his thick, dark hair. "Got something for you." He reached into his back pocket, his muscles dancing as he pulled forth a second identical cap. "Free with a purchase of semigloss."

Abbie laughed and crawled over the passenger side to exit. She slammed the door, her feet never noticing the difference from gravel to grass; her attention was riveted solely on him. "Why, thanks. I've never had anyone give me a painter's cap for a gift before." Taking the cardboard brim, she bent it between her thumbs before jauntily cocking it on an off angle at the back of her head. "I'll treasure it always."

He gave the brim a quick tug. "There. Better."

She rolled her eyes, then posed as if she was modeling a turn-of-the-century hat. "And how's the paint?" she drawled, batting her eyelashes. "Are we still doing piña colada?"

"We are. I just finished trimming the window."

"What?" The posturing wilted. "You started without me?"

"If we get done early, we can linger over the apple pie I picked up at the bakery. You said it was your favorite."

Disbelief washed over her. "You remembered?"

"It fits, Ab. You're as all-American as apple pie. Who can forget that?"

The nonchalant yet tender way he said it hit a soft spot in Abbie. Nobody had ever paid much attention to what she liked. She'd grown used to it, accepted it.

She choked over the way he made her feel special. Yet this was a thank-you for helping out, nothing more, she told herself fiercely. "You didn't have to go out of your way for that," she said. "I'd have brought dessert."

"You think the only reason I invited you was to take advantage of your way with a paintbrush?" He didn't give her time to answer. "Not true. The truth is, I want to take advantage of your way with *me*. Play with my mind, Abbie, over apple pie and coffee."

"Aha! So you're using me as an experiment."

For a moment, his smile faded and his dimples disappeared. "I am. I admit it."

She chuckled. Then still wearing her paint cap, Abbie grabbed Jack's hand and pulled him into the house behind her. They got right down to work, but the good feelings and the banter escalated.

When the opposite two walls they'd started on converged, they met each other, thigh to thigh in the bathtub, each wielding a paint roller.

The atmosphere dramatically changed.

"Oops. Sorry."

"Here. Let me move over."

"I'm okay. You have enough room?"

"Oh, fine. Fine," Abbie lied.

They painted side by side for several minutes of awkward silence. Then Abbie couldn't stand it another second. She bit her lip. Then she started to laugh.

"What?"

"Nothing."

"What?" he prompted again, the paint roller dropping between them.

"I just realized this is a first. I've never been in a bathtub with a man before."

Jack grinned, his attention drifting down to her chin. He leaned over the edge of the bathtub to lay the roller in the tray. As he straightened, he pulled a rag from his back pocket and carefully dabbed at her chin, then at a spot beneath her lashes. "You're getting paint all over you," he said huskily. "I thought you said you knew how to do this."

Abbie stood paralyzed as he ministered to her. The porcelain ribs of the bathtub floor rolled beneath her stocking feet. They leaned toward each other as if a gravitational pull had somehow tightened its hold on them.

Her paint roller wavered, narrowly missing the front of his overalls.

"Better let me have that," he said, casually extracting

the handle from her and putting it down next to his. "Now. Where were we?"

Abbie's gaze drifted to his mouth. "About how I was making a mess of this, I think."

"You aren't making a mess of anything, Abbie."

Her gaze drifted lower. To the perfect cut of his chin, to his strong neck and the speckles of paint that created a sensuality over his bare shoulders. He was so, so perfect. And she was standing fully clothed in a bathtub with him. The soap dish, screwed to the wall, hit the side of her knee.

"Jack—"

"Shh. Don't move." The pad of his thumb returned to her cheek. "I didn't get it all," he whispered.

Abbie held her breath, aware all her senses were at fever pitch. The scents of turpentine and soap and stale aftershave were like an aphrodisiac.

"There." His knuckles traced the curve of her jaw.

Warm sparks fluttered through her, drifting over her breasts and down through her middle, then lower, where desire curled and beckoned. In one sane moment, it struck her how isolated they were.

They were alone here in this big old house with no one knowing and nothing but their mismatched feelings.

Risk. Opportunity. Both taunted her.

"The bathroom's almost done," she said unnecessarily.

"Like I care," he replied hoarsely, his shoulders hunching down, and his eyes drifting closed as his mouth moved within inches of her own. "Come here."

They embraced, her arms splicing beneath his, her fingertips sliding under the overall straps to trace the shell-like blades of his shoulders. Perspiration dampened his skin.

He groaned, instinctively drawing her up against him. "Abbie, how can you look so damn sexy with a paint roller in your hand?"

"You don't have to say things like that, Jack." She

turned her face up, expecting the kiss she so desperately sought.

He imperceptibly pulled back, his blue gaze quizzically locking with her dark one. "Don't have to...?"

"I'd feel just the same anyway."

He frowned, then dipped his head. "Forget it," he muttered, moving toward her mouth. "I don't know who's trying to prove what to whom anymore."

The telephone rang at that very moment, snapping them apart.

"Damn," he swore.

Abbie self-consciously yanked down her sweatshirt.

He chuckled, watching her. "Hey. It's only the phone."

"I know. Go answer it."

Jack stepped out of the bathtub with enough momentum to have jerked the cord free from the wall jack. "Yeah?"

Dead silence.

Then, "What do you want?"

Abbie stood alone in the bathtub, listening and feeling remarkably foolish for doing so. She idly picked up Jack's paint roller because she wanted to get the feel of it. Dipping it in the paint, she swiped at a tiny spot near the shower head. As she touched up their work, she heard every monosyllabic reply he uttered.

Finally, "So how'd you get my phone number?" Three beats of silence. "Because it's none of your business."

Abbie dawdled at the spot where piña colada met ceiling white.

"Forget it, Rob. Don't call. Don't ask."

The rising inflection of his voice made Abbie feel like an eavesdropper. Laying the roller aside, she carefully stepped out of the tub and padded across the hall to skim down the back steps. Once in the kitchen, she automatically reached into the cupboards to help herself to plates and forks. It was comforting to put the coffee on to perk.

Domesticity was her strong suit. It fortified her, gave her

the strength to know what to say, to know how to make people relax.

The atmosphere had already changed; she could feel it. It wasn't so different from all those years ago when, without any rhyme or reason, her mother would fly into her room and slam the door. She remembered tiptoeing around the house and leaving trays of tea and cookies on the floor next to her mother's door; the disappointment when they went untouched; the jubilance when they were accepted.

She sliced the pie, careful that every crumb of the Dutch topping stayed on the wedge, cautious that she didn't break the crust. Tamping down her nervousness, she cocked her head to listen.

Nothing.

Napkins, she told herself. She needed napkins. Finding two in soothing pastels, she folded them in perfect triangles and placed a fork over each.

The comforts of home would take his mind off his trouble. He had a stressful job, she told herself. His life was stressful. People didn't leave him alone. Everyone wanted a piece of him.

The receiver slammed against the cradle and, given the noise, Abbie winced, thinking he must have kicked Ma Bell all the way across the room.

The evening, and all the good feelings, were gone. He stomped overhead to the bathroom, then across the hall and down the steps. When he came into the room, his mouth was a thin, hard line.

"So. Everything okay?"

"Just peachy," he said, jerking a chair away from the table.

"Coffee?" He didn't answer but gave Abbie a glimpse of tense shoulders, a set jaw. "Maybe something stronger?"

His head swiveled, but he looked at her blankly.

"I'm sorry. You're probably not ready for the pie yet. I shouldn't have—"

"Don't apologize," he snapped. "And for God's sake, don't wait on me. If I want coffee, I'm perfectly capable of getting it myself."

Direct hit.

Abbie's efforts, her intentions, dissolved like a teaspoon of sugar in a Colombian blend.

"I'm sorry. I didn't mean to pry. I—"

"You're doing it again!"

"What?"

"Apologizing. Would you quit?" At her stricken expression, he softened, slumping back against the chair. "I should be apologizing to you."

"For what?" She pushed herself off the counter and moved farther into the room.

"For my temper. For criticizing. You're just that way and I should know it." He sighed heavily. "But just quit, will you? Don't even ask."

Abbie stopped short, all the uncertain questions trapped in her throat.

He must have known how he'd closed her down. "Look, I'm not dragging you into this, Abbie. I'm not. It's old stuff, left over from Omaha. I'm putting it behind me. Without anyone's help. Certainly without yours."

"Okay."

"But I'm sorry for it. And I'm sorry it ruined the evening." He sadly eyed the perfectly set table. "One phone call took the spice right out of the pie, didn't it?"

"Doesn't matter, Jack. Really."

He ground the heel of his hand against his left eye, then dragged his splayed fingers through his hair. "Like hell it doesn't."

"If you want me to leave—"

"I don't!"

She stared at him, speechless. He'd raised his voice, handed out orders and snubbed her concern.

"Look, I have to tell you, Abbie, I don't have a lot left to give. Whatever happens between us is the here and now. Not the future, not the past. You may as well know from the beginning there are some things I refuse to include you in. And that's just the way it is."

"If it's your work—"

"It isn't. But no matter what, you better remember it always comes first."

Abbie looked at him, purposely ignoring what he said. "Then what happened in the ER, Jack?"

"Not a damn thing! Just eighteen-hour shifts of splicing and dicing body parts. And the helluva poor personal life that went along with it."

Abbie winced, her features crumpling.

"Forget what I said," he muttered. "I came back to Cooper to get away from all that, not to rehash it."

"You were the one who—"

"I know. Okay? But every time I'm reminded of how Rob made my life a nightmare, something bursts inside me."

"Who is this...this Rob?" Abbie lifted her hands, palm side up.

"The person who single-handedly controlled my life." Jack sank back, his fist hitting the table before he seared her with eyes of blue ice. "And now," he said determinedly, "it's over. By God, it's over."

Chapter Eight

There was only one explanation for Jack's behavior, Abbie finally concluded four days later as she organized the workroom in her new building. Burnout. He'd worked long hours in Omaha, under stressful conditions, and he'd experienced tragic accidents, horrible deaths. He wouldn't tell her, but she surmised Rob was most likely someone he'd worked with, a superior, perhaps another doctor.

That *had* to be it. Burnout, and a difficult co-worker.

Jack needed normalcy in his life, and if there was anything Abbie was capable of providing another human being, it was that.

Twenty years ago, when her mother had run off, Abbie had consciously commandeered her family into keeping up the routines. She had chided her sisters—and occasionally her father—into doing what was expected of them. It had been a rough time, one that left them scarred, bruising their idealistic bird's-eye view of love, trust and commitment.

During those first few ugly months, her father lost his easy smile and spent hours brooding or working out in the fields until long after dark. Her sisters, sullen and angry, picked at each other.

It was Abbie who put the meals on the table, who took care of the wash, the house and the groceries. By the time she was nine years old, she knew how to toil like an old woman, always with nagging thoughts.

She had wanted answers that would put walls around the unknown.

Finally, she could stand it no longer, and on a sunny July day, while her father raked alfalfa, she'd walked his sack lunch out to the fields. She'd never forget how he'd leaned against the black rubber tractor tire, crossing his boots in front of him as he poured lemonade from the thermos. She had watched it swirl into the bottom of the red plastic cup, knowing he would share it with her.

The questions were out of her mouth before she could think about it.

Did Mama leave because she doesn't love us?

You know better than that, Boo. Sure she loves you.

Is she ever coming back?

I don't know! Don't ask me, dammit. It's not up to me. I'm as helpless as anyone.

Abbie, who'd been sent away without the lemonade, had suffered a valuable lesson that day: people don't talk about the pain in their lives, not until they're ready to.

She imagined it was the same with Jack.

But I'll never forgive her, Abbie thought unexpectedly as she jammed paper shred into cardboard bins, *because she took too much of our lives away with her. We sacrificed everything and ended up clinging to each other, filling ourselves up with self-doubt and insecurities. I hate her for what she's done to us, for what she's made of us. I want more than anything to love Jack, but now, because of her, I don't know if I can.*

Abbie had grown up vowing that, unlike her mother, her love would be patient, kind and unconditional. Yet after the first storm she and Jack had endured, her fears spiraled. What if her mother's desertion had stunted her emotionally? What if she wasn't capable of loving a man, not the way a woman should?

Despite her misgivings, she knew only one thing: when Jack was ready to open up, she'd be there for him. It was all she could do. In the meantime, she'd accept his tight-lipped silence.

It was a small price to pay for all he'd given her.

They fell into a comfortable routine. Abbie worked on putting the building in order; Jack thrived on predictable working hours. In between, they spent every free hour together.

"So, here it is. What do you think?" Jack unrolled a length of teal border trim.

Abbie couldn't help herself. She reached out, tracing the gold filigree running through the pattern. "Stunning."

"You think? Not too much for the dining room?"

"Absolutely not."

He pushed a stack of mail aside to unfold the paint-chip chart. "I'm going to have to go custom again."

"Imagine it, Jack. Your grandfather and custom-painted walls. You know what he'd say, don't you?"

"Yeah. 'Just slap on a coat of that mismixed stuff Gordon sells for two bucks a can. It'll do the job.'"

His imitation, right down to the sandpapery growl that had once been Gramps's trademark, was priceless. Abbie grinned, wondering if all South Dakota ranchers were pried, kicking and screaming, out of the same frugal mold.

She shook her head, glancing at the mess on the table. Wallpaper books, carpet samples, vinyl and tile, stir sticks, drop cloths. A paint tray and brush lay over a week's worth of collected mail.

Then the letters caught her eye. The Omaha return address. The taped label in the upper-left corner of dozens of envelopes.

Rob Stearling.

A queasy feeling pitched through Abbie's stomach. The letters were unopened; Jack always slit the flaps with a letter opener.

She scanned the dates. September 14, 12, 19 and 22. Several others, with October dates, were half-hidden beneath flyers and newspapers, but the familiar return-address label jumped out at her, mocking her.

"Hey. You listening?" Jack asked, nudging her.

Abbie fought to collect herself. God, she didn't want to be caught gaping at his mail. "Sure, I am...but..." She leaned over his arm, barely aware her breast was pressing against it.

His blunt-cut fingernail tapped a deep, vibrant color. Peacock blue. "Well?"

"Yes," she said decisively. "It's a big room. You can get away with it."

"I knew you'd say that. I already ordered it."

"Then why bother to ask?"

"To reassure myself."

"Like you need reassurance on your choices."

He looked at her keenly, the back of his arm chafing her breasts as he turned. "Can you stay?"

She hesitated. God knows she wanted to. She didn't want to miss so much as a minute with Jack. "I'd better not. Daddy's expecting me."

"Oh."

She noted the disappointment in his voice, surprised by it. "Well, I would, but he's been kind of funny lately. Mad and short-tempered at everything I do. It's not like him. Maybe it's all the time I'm spending on the building, maybe it's—"

"Me?"

"Oh, no. I don't think so." But, unable to vehemently deny it, she straightened. "He knows we're just friends."

Jack arched a disbelieving eyebrow.

"Old friends," she revised too quickly.

"Is that what you're telling him?"

"What should I say? You're going back to Omaha in a couple of months."

"I know. But still…" He flipped the paint chart onto the table. "He isn't complaining of any physical symptoms, is he? Maybe he should come see me."

"Daddy? You know him, strong as a horse. Does the work of two men and always finds time to scare up more."

"Abbie, he's getting up there."

"He's not sick, Jack."

"Maybe not." Jack picked up Abbie's hand, making the simple gesture the most natural, most thrilling thing in the world. This was not sex, nor passion, but tenderness.

Companionable silence settled in.

Abbie's heart lodged in her throat. She swallowed, fearful of breaking the moment.

"And maybe you're right. Maybe it's not me," he said, his thumb and forefinger exploring each of her four digits. "Maybe it's you. He's losing his little girl, Abbie. You're growing up and away from him. The new business, the busy schedule. It's taking you away. Maybe he's not ready for it."

"He's put up with me for almost thirty years, Jack. I'd think he'd want to be rid of me."

Jack grinned, his grasp tightening. "I don't think so."

For the first time, without an invitation, Abbie spontaneously folded herself into Jack's arms. She shivered, hoping he wouldn't notice.

"You spoil him, Boo."

"I know. But he deserves it. He's always been there for me."

"Huh. Like father, like daughter." He stroked the wispy

ends of her hair before pulling his head back to meet her gaze. "Like you've been here for me."

Abbie's lips curved at the corners. "Thanks for saying it."

"No, I mean it."

Her forehead dropped to the hollow of his shoulder. "You know," she said slowly, "even if you're wrong about Daddy, it's nice having you say someone loves me, that someone loves me enough not to want to let go. After Mom left, I never thought anyone would love me that much, not ever again."

Abbie couldn't see it, but Jack's mouth thinned and his eyes closed tightly.

The first full day Abbie planned to work at the shop, she asked Jack to come for lunch. Rather than getting the showroom in order as she should have, she spent the entire morning making sure everything was picture-perfect. Fresh fruit in a cut-glass bowl, veggies on a platter. Iced tea with lemon wedges.

At five minutes after twelve, the brass bell she'd hung over the front door jangled. Abbie poked her head around the doorway separating the workroom from the showroom.

"Hey. We still on?" Jack, who usually sported a white lab coat, wore a scarlet-colored golf shirt. From the pocket of his dress pants hung the ear tips of a stethoscope.

Abbie smiled at him. "Of course. Come on in. Sirloin over rice, fresh fruit and veggies."

He gaped at her. "Are you kidding? I was expecting tuna salad."

"We need to break this place in right." She tilted her head, indicating the extravagant table nestled cozily in the bay window. Black-rimmed china adorned with pale pink and lavender irises sat on fuchsia linen. Stuffed inside the clear, black-stemmed water goblets were matching fanfolded fuchsia napkins. A bouquet of carnations, in brilliant shades of pink and purple, mingled with baby's breath.

"Abbie...this looks like seduction instead of lunch."

Color inched up her neck.

"I only wanted to do something special," she protested. "For the first time."

He looked away, grinning, his dimples popping into place as if she'd said something outrageously funny. "I thought we'd eat upstairs or out on the back porch." He pulled out a folding chair and stuffed the stethoscope deeper into his pocket before sitting.

Abbie peeled plastic wrap off the vegetable tray, then put a spoon in the fruit. "The upstairs is pretty dismal. The plaster's cracked and the whole place reminds me of a sweatshop. Don't you think this is better?" she asked, placing matching china casserole dishes on the table.

He lifted both lids. "Abbie. This is incredible."

She beamed, self-consciously sliding into the opposite chair. "We've got cheesecake for dessert."

"You're waiting on me," he chided. "I was expecting casual. A can of soda and cheap paper plates."

Abbie glanced around, suddenly seeing the absurd setting through his eyes: the tablecloth, the flowers, the china. The extravagant food, including out-of-season watermelon, artichoke hearts and tiny ears of gourmet pickled corn. "It's too obvious," she said flatly. "I overdid it."

Uneasy silence followed, then, under the table, Jack nudged her knee. "It's wonderful. I've never been so flattered."

"Great. You feel flattered, and I've just made a fool of myself."

"Abbie! It's you. It's special. Only you would knock yourself out to create an illusion this spectacular."

Illusion? Abbie winced. "Are you laughing at me for botching this one?"

"Botching it? Are you kidding?" He took her hand.

"From here on out, I'll never be able to look at tuna salad and call it lunch again. You, my dear Boo, have just upped my expectations."

"Jack—"

The bell over the front door jangled, and they both turned, Abbie's hand still tucked into Jack's.

A blond, brawny man strode through the front door, letting his blue eyes roll over Jack. "Hey, man, how are you? So this is where you've been hiding out!" Spying their entwined grasp, his full lips split into a grin. "Intimate, Jack. Very intimate."

"Eklund! What're you doin' here?"

"Meeting a bunch of guys for a fishing trip into Canada. One last go before the snow flies. I was so close I had to stop and look in on you."

"I'll be damned." Jack stood, flipping the napkin off his lap as he tugged on Abbie's fingers to pull her up beside him. "Hey, I want you to meet someone."

Their guest chortled. "So you finally caught up with her, huh? Good move. I swear, she looks the same as those pictures you flashed!"

Abbie's mouth went dry.

There was no mistaking his meaning. None whatsoever. Natalie. He assumed she was Natalie.

Abbie jerked her hand free, feeling a pang of jealousy, of hurt. But Eklund, who was now taking in the romantic table for two, winked broadly at Jack.

"Abigail Worth," she clarified, stiffly extending her hand. "Not Natalie. Not Meredith. Sorry about the confusion, but my sisters and I all bear a striking resemblance."

The jovial mood faltered.

"Oh, I—I just figured you were the one from high school."

"I am. But not *the* one. We're triplets. There were three of us to choose from in high school."

Jack visibly blanched, then lifted a helpless shoulder.

"I'm making more respectable choices now. My tastes have changed. Considerably." With forced calm, he added, "Abbie, I want you to meet Anders Eklund. We shared the horrors of med school together."

"How nice. Let me get another plate." Abbie tossed her napkin beside her plate.

"Oh, no. No, I can't stay."

But Abbie, humiliated, didn't listen; she turned away to get it anyway.

Jack caught her arm, pulling her back up and close against him. She had no alternative but to face Anders and his curiosity. "Those were old prom photos you remember of Nat," he said. "I made the same mistake my first day back. But, believe me, Abbie and Nat are as different as night and day. I'd never make that mistake all over again."

Eklund read into the double meaning, his eyes shifting from Jack to Abbie and back again.

Abbie escaped Jack's possessive hold. "Please. Let me set another plate," she offered without a hint of graciousness. "You've driven all this way and there's more than enough."

She scrounged up another chair, and they made room for Eklund's bulk at the card table. Both men ate ravenously, peppering the strained conversation with compliments. To his credit, Jack strove to carry off the lunch; Abbie, after tamping down the welling hurt, reminded herself to behave like a lady.

After one o'clock, Jack reluctantly pushed back from the table, saying he had a waiting room full of patients. "I've got to go."

"Well, it was good to see you, man. Looks like you're all settled in, bein' a country doctor."

"I am."

"Looks good on you."

Abbie started cleaning up, but Jack took the plate out of

Here's a **HOT** offer for you!

Get set for a sizzling summer read...

with **2 FREE ROMANCE BOOKS** and a **FREE MYSTERY GIFT!**

NO CATCH! NO OBLIGATION TO BUY!

Simply complete and return this card and you'll get **FREE BOOKS, A FREE GIFT** and much more!

- ● The first shipment is yours to keep, **absolutely free!**
- ● Enjoy the convenience of romance books, delivered right to your door, before they're available in the stores!
- ● Take advantage of special low pricing for **Reader Service Members only!**
- ● After receiving your free books we hope you'll want to remain a subscriber. But the choice is always yours—to continue or cancel anytime at all! So why not take us up on this fabulous invitation with no risk of any kind. You'll be glad you did!

315 SDL CPSQ

215 SDL CPSH
S-R-05/99

▶ DETACH HERE AND MAIL CARD TODAY! ▶

Name:	
	(Please Print)
Address:	Apt.#:
City:	
State/Prov.:	Zip/ Postal Code:

The Silhouette Reader Service™ —Here's How it Works:

Accepting your 2 free books and mystery gift places you under no obligation to buy anything. You may keep the books and gift and return the shipping statement marked "cancel." If you do not cancel, about a month later we'll send you 6 additional novels and bill you just $2.90 each in the U.S., or $3.25 each in Canada, plus 25¢ delivery per book and applicable taxes if any.* That's the complete price and — compared to the cover price of $3.50 in the U.S. and $3.99 in Canada — it's quite a bargain! You may cancel at any time, but if you choose to continue, every month we'll send you 6 more books, which you may either purchase at the discount price or return to us and cancel your subscription.

*Terms and prices subject to change without notice. Sales tax applicable in N.Y. Canadian residents will be charged applicable provincial taxes and GST.

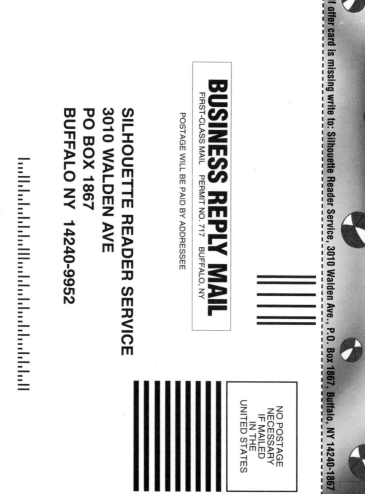

If offer card is missing write to: Silhouette Reader Service, 3010 Walden Ave., P.O. Box 1867, Buffalo, NY 14240-1867

BUSINESS REPLY MAIL
FIRST-CLASS MAIL   PERMIT NO. 717   BUFFALO, NY

POSTAGE WILL BE PAID BY ADDRESSEE

SILHOUETTE READER SERVICE
3010 WALDEN AVE
PO BOX 1867
BUFFALO NY 14240-9952

NO POSTAGE
NECESSARY
IF MAILED
IN THE
UNITED STATES

her hand. "Leave that," he insisted. "I'll do the dishes tonight. Come on, Boo. Walk out with us."

He guided her across the street to Eklund's 4X4 parked in front of his office. They tarried at the opened driver's-side door.

"Thanks for stopping by." Jack shook his friend's hand before giving him a bear hug. "Good to see you again. You always were full of surprises."

"Yeah. And I sure managed one today, huh?" When Jack chuckled, he opened the door and reached inside. "The thing is, it doesn't stop there, either," Eklund said, his back to them both. "Got hoodwinked into bringing something along for you." He passed a magnum of champagne, the bottle neck beribboned with a dozen coiling metallic streamers, and a card attached with a gigantic bow, to Jack. "For you. A peace offering from Rob."

Jack's expression shuttered, and he threw his arm around Abbie. "Thanks, but no thanks."

"Hey. Take it, will you? This time, she claims she's sending her apologies."

She? Abbie's knees buckled, and she swayed in surprise. Jack steadied her, his arm gripping her more firmly.

"Take it. Feed the fishies. Or pass it around the campfire. But tell her I said no. To everything."

Eklund tilted the magnum, inspecting the pricey label. "Okay. Whatever you say, man. You know me, always happy to suck up your leftovers."

A wry smile turned up Jack's lips.

Eklund tossed the elaborately dressed bottle next to him on the seat and slid in. He threw the 4X4 in gear, then slapped a baseball cap on his head before stepping on the accelerator. Before he left, his meaty hand offered a congenial salute via the side mirror.

Neither Jack nor Abbie moved. They stared after his rear bumper until it was little more than a speck on the highway heading out of town.

"Jack—"

"I don't want to talk about it, Abbie. Not now. I've patients waiting and I've ruined lunch. We'll hammer this out later."

But a multitude of questions seesawed through Abbie's brain, doing a hatchet job on what was left of her composure. "You convinced me you came back to Cooper because of the job, not Natalie. And I thought Rob Stearling was someone you worked with—a *man* you worked with—and—"

"I came back to Cooper, Abbie, because, corny as it sounds, I wanted to come home again. I wanted all the comforts of small-town life. I thought that would fix it all."

"And the woman?"

"Rob Stearling? Okay. She was once my fiancée, Abbie."

Chapter Nine

Jack left her standing in the street with her mouth hanging open, feeling foolish and used and dispensable. The leftover food, by the time she got back to it, was cold and withered. Dismissing his offer to clean up, she plunged into the job. Having her hands in a sink full of soapy dishwater was cleansing to her soul. Tearing down the table and chairs used up her ferocious energy.

Thinking time, that's what it was.

Honest answers, that's all she wanted from him! He'd certainly gone out of his way to neglect telling her a few details about his ten-year hiatus from Cooper. A fiancée! One he'd never even mentioned?

And that business about Natalie! What did he think? That he was going to come waltzing back into her life and pick up where they'd left off?

When Jack locked the door of the doctor's office at 5:35, Abbie was ready for him. She met him at the front door of her shop and held it open, putting her shoulder against the frame. She couldn't trust herself to say one word.

At the same time, she memorized everything about him,

figuring this would be the last time they'd be together. The
casual swing of his gait, the creases in his chino pants, the
glint of the gold watch circling his wrist. His hair, in the
late afternoon, as it reflected a blue-black brilliance.

It had been a wonderful run. She should be thankful for
that much. He'd added a new dimension to her life, one
that had changed her, enriched her.

He strode up the three porch treads, making no move to
cross the threshold. He was so gorgeous that, for a moment,
her legs trembled.

Pausing, then looking like a man with his hat in his
hands, he said, "You forgive me yet?"

She let a second slip away. "Hearing it that way was
quite a shock, Jack."

"I know."

Abbie's heart thudded in her chest. "It didn't have to
happen like that. You could have told me. About Rob.
About how you felt about Nat."

"That's the thing, Abbie. I don't feel anything for Nat.
When I left Omaha, I wanted to, that's all." Jack scraped
his loafer over the step. "Sure, I guess I wanted to know
if there could be any more *us,* if there was anything left to
resurrect a relationship with."

"You'd have to ask her. Not me." She weathered his
stare, his eyes flicking over her hair, her chin, her temples.
"Because I can't answer that for you."

"You already have." His eyes narrowed thoughtfully,
the blue color briefly disappearing. "I found something I
far prefer to Natalie's whims, something far more fascinating than her flighty high school flirtations." He hesitated,
his expression solemn, his cheeks, without the dimples, flat
and smooth. "I found you, Abbie."

The revelation unnerved her, but she refused to show it.
"If you're saying that because you think you've hurt me,
or because I found out about Nat and this Rob, or—"

"It's all I've thought about the whole afternoon. I picked

up the phone twice to call you. There I was, kids screaming in the office, and Mrs. Dillon freezing under a paper sheet in the examining room, and I put everything on hold to call you.''

Abbie tried to imagine it. ''What could you possibly have said to me?''

''That I'm sorry.'' Abbie looked away over his shoulder, wondering how—or if—she could forgive so easily. ''That I meant to tell you. Someday.''

''I feel like I've been blindsided.''

''You've a right to feel that way.''

''If you'd only asked about Natalie. I'd have realized—''

''How? How could I have done it kindly? And anyway, after a while it didn't matter. I didn't care.''

''Aw, Jack…''

''Aw, Jack, what?''

She opened the door a smidgen wider. ''Come in. We need to talk.''

''Am I winning you over, Boo?''

''You just may be.''

He stepped inside, his arm brushing hers to open a floodgate of longing. His back was to the bare spot where the card table had stood earlier that afternoon. It was all she could do to beat back her feelings, to remain expressionless.

''Will you accept my apology, Abbie?'' The muscle along his jawline twitched.

''It would probably be best to simply say yes, wouldn't it?''

''No. Because I'd like you to mean it.''

Abbie vacillated, painfully aware there were some things about Natalie she could never divulge. But perhaps she could soften the disappointment. ''I forgive you, Jack. But you should know Natalie isn't the same person you remember.''

''What do I care about that?''

''She had a tough time getting through college. Experiences that changed her. But she's happy now. She's got a new job in Rapid City and a boyfriend called Carl something or other.''

"I don't give a fig about Nat or where she is and what she's doing.''

"Right. But in the back of your mind, you're probably wondering—''

"I'm not.''

"She's the one with the fire, Jack.''

"And you're not?''

"Fire?'' She snorted. "Hardly. No. Maybe a slow burn.''

He chuckled, his eyes squinting into delectable crescents. "You're right, Boo. You've got lasting power. You're much too smart, too well tempered to lose it in a big poof of flame.'' One tremulous heartbeat slipped away. "You're an incredible woman, Abbie.''

When the full import of his statement hit Abbie, she stared, the muscles holding up her mouth, her chin, going slack. No one in her whole life had ever considered her incredible. She was Abbie, the one who caused ripples, not waves.

"Jack...there's a lot about me you don't know.''

"I'd jump at the chance to learn.''

He'd put her at a crossroads. The choice was up to her.

Abbie debated, then silently, slowly, turned the sign on the front door over to Closed. "I fixed some iced tea,'' she offered. "We could check out the sweatshop upstairs. You could tell me that story about your fiancée.''

He smiled grimly. "I think it's about time.''

He followed her up the narrow staircase at the back of the building into an expanse of dull white walls and high ceilings. Abbie pulled a pitcher from the apartment-size fridge, and Jack dropped onto one of the two huge pillows beneath the Main Street windows.

It was a rattletrap apartment with possibilities. It smelled dusty and unused, the empty, cavernous room echoing their footsteps. After offering him a tumbler of tea, Abbie sank onto the pillow beside him.

"I met Robin Stearling the year before med school," Jack said without preamble. "She was a news reporter, one who loved being 'on.' Everywhere we went, she was recognized."

"You liked that?"

"Sometimes," he said honestly, balancing his glass on his knee. "We were together all through med school, and to be fair, she helped me survive it. Six years," he mused, tipping his head back against the wall. "At first we planned to get married—but later we came up with a dozen excuses to never get around to it. My internship. Her job. I got so I liked it that way. She said she did, too."

"And then?"

"I broke it off." He drew a deep breath. "I wanted to come home at night to a house, not an apartment. I wanted to throw hot dogs on the grill and have a beer. Rob wanted dinner out, opera tickets and an appearance at the local hot spot. Those things were good for her career, hell on mine."

Abbie imagined the differences.

"One night, I was paged for a medical emergency, and Rob was furious. We ended up in one of those five-minute fights. You know, the kind that makes your blood pressure feel like it's going right out the top of your head?"

Shuttering her eyes, Abbie nodded.

"Rob said the only thing that would make her marry me was the M.D. following my name. It would get her into the country club where she could schmooze with the Junior League."

"Oh, Jack…"

"Hey. No contest between me or my M.D. The degree won hands down. So I packed up and moved out."

"So that's why you came back here."

He frowned at her. "Abbie, this relationship has been over with for a long time. Over two years. Rob had a few second thoughts and wanted to patch things up, but I knew it was a dead-end relationship. She doesn't get it. You heard me on the phone with her. Don't tell me you haven't seen that stack of letters.''

Abbie guiltily lifted her eyebrows before poking the lemon wedge farther down into her iced tea.

"It's like I'm being stalked, and I'm tired of being nice about it. I want out.''

"Maybe you need to make it clear to her—'' Abbie swallowed, aware she intended to advise him in a way that would benefit her ''—that it's over.''

"It *is* over. It's been over. But Rob makes me feel like I'm trying to explain a mathematical equation with a crayon on a square of toilet tissue. She doesn't get it.''

"So you thought you'd get away from her with a new fling in your old hometown.''

He grinned, not grasping her full meaning. "Nothing wrong with that, is there?''

"That depends. On whom it involves.''

His amusement faded. "Abbie, I'd never do anything to hurt you. Not after what I've been through. Rob's made my life hell. She's smothered me in cards and letters. She's followed me home from the hospital and haunted my favorite restaurants. She's even said she's ready to be a wife and mother.''

"She said that?''

"Oh, forget it. For her, marriage and kids are only the by-products of the life she wants. Being away from her made me see that. I don't love her. I never did.''

Abbie grew pensive, unable to fathom how this woman had abused her own fantasy of a life with Jack. "How do you plan to get her out of your life?'' she asked.

"I don't know. It doesn't look like long distance is going to do it.''

"They say absence makes the heart grow fonder.''

Annoyance furrowed his brow, and he swiped at the

moisture forming on the side of his glass. "No, but Rob's a menace. She's tainted me. She needs to be put down for souring me on marriage and the all-American family. From here on out, all I want is a good time. Forget the commitments."

Something in the area of Abbie's heart fluttered, then flickered into mute, agonizing despair.

Insulation grew around Abbie like frost on a window. She started timing her moves to avoid Jack instead of meeting him. That was easy to do because, in the middle of October, he was swamped with cold and flu shots, winter-sports physicals and snowbirds who wanted early appointments. She likewise threw herself into her holiday preparations, ticking them off as methodically as her mind reeled off arguments about Jack.

Autumn baskets: Halloween and Thanksgiving. Christmas giftware, both prepackaged and custom.

Jack came back because of Natalie.

A loose-leaf catalogue customers could thumb through. Order blanks. Business cards with her new address. Pamphlets.

Jack stuffed his secrets into his back pocket, hiding them.

Balloons for the grand opening. Drop cookies, lemonade and coffee for refreshments. Baskets for hourly prize drawings.

His old flame, Rob Stearling, was determined to win Jack back into her lair.

Abbie's enthusiasm over the shop waned, the hard work potholed with thoughts that repeatedly strayed to her problems with Jack. Even her father was becoming a nuisance. At the same time she was slaving away on her building, he started coming up with ideas to fix up the ranch house.

Like she had time. Like she cared.

The only thing she cared about was her foolish notion

that she could put her heart on the line for a few memories to cherish. That wasn't possible.

After Jack scoffed at his romantic folly with Rob, she saw the risk. She was setting herself up for another failed relationship, too similar to the one she'd shared with her mother: loving someone who couldn't love her in return.

That would destroy her; it would undermine the last shred of her self-worth.

The lost child she had once disguised resurfaced. Everything reminded her of what she'd done to drive her fears, her inadequacies, away. The cookies she had baked, the good deeds she had racked up, her generosity and stoic smile. Everything, including her building's false-fronted exterior, reminded her of the misery she kept hidden in her lonely heart.

She didn't think she could bear it anymore.

She had to make some changes and she had to make them now. They would be profound and honest, born of the wisdom she had earned.

Chapter Ten

The morning of Abbie's official open house dawned brilliant and clear, and with the tang of winter in the air, she piled the last of her baskets and boxes into the car. Not expecting to see Jack, she yanked on her old jacket.

It had been two weeks since their disastrous lunch date. The heart-to-heart they'd shared in the apartment over the showroom, sitting on pillows with nothing stronger than iced tea between them, had apparently prompted Jack to backpedal, too.

It bothered her. She didn't want it that way. But then, perhaps he realized he had willfully taken their relationship outside the parameters of friendship.

As she drove, her mind conjured up all kinds of images. The way he patted his breast pocket, absently checking to make sure he hadn't lost his prescription pad. The way the ear tips on his stethoscope inched out of his pants pocket. The lab coats she'd seen hanging in his closet. How they smelled, all cleaned and starched—like sunshine with a dollop of bleach.

She would really miss those details in her life.

He would know today was her grand opening because she'd broken down last night and left a message on his answering machine, reminding him. She'd never gotten a reply, leaving her to assume he would be too busy to stop in.

No matter, she told herself as she pulled up behind the building, cringing as all the boxes in the back seat pitched forward. Their friendship would only survive if she went on with her life. Climbing out of her car, Abbie buttoned up her jacket and got to work.

Her father claimed she'd worked miracles with the first floor showroom. It was a trendy but nostalgic display. One corner highlighted her dad's old corn sheller, with baskets of corn relish, jellies and jams, honey and syrups, piled around it. Across the aisle three beat-up sleds she'd salvaged from the barn were skirted with crumpled tinfoil and garlands. Gift-giving novelties were in baskets covered with red and green cellophane.

In the back, her father had fastened tiny shelves to the old cream separator. On that, Abbie displayed her custom gift-giving suggestions.

Everything was perfect. Not one greeting card nor piece of paper shred out of place. Chairs were arranged informally. Business cards and flyers discreetly placed on adjacent tables. The punch was at the back of the room so her guests had to wander through the maze she'd created before they got to the watering hole.

Her first visitors were browsers who stopped merely to put in an appearance or catch a snippet of gossip. They wanted to walk away from the new business in town, form an opinion of it, then say they were there when it opened.

Kids yanked on the strings of their free balloons while women oohed and aahed over the merchandise and nursed paper cups of lemonade. Men straggled in only because they hoped to talk with her dad—but he'd begged off because of a previous commitment, one he'd been peculiarly vague about.

Abbie, disappointed her father hadn't come, presumed he didn't want to endure the hoopla and let it go at that. She'd do this. Even if she had to do it alone.

Then the bombshell dropped.

Jack strolled in during his lunch hour, a huge shopping bag at his side. He glad-handed his way past several guests, then pointedly made his way toward her.

Abbie's face flushed when the gossip died down to whispers and everyone craned their necks. In Cooper, it was hard to keep romance a secret. "Hi," she said a little too cheerfully. "What can I get you, Jack? A cup of lemonade?"

He smiled, appearing unaffected by the crowd he'd drawn. "A gift basket?"

"All right." She walked around to the makeshift counter, the one her father had fashioned in his toolshed.

"I've got some goodies here. Lots of them. And I'd like them all packaged and hand delivered."

"Okay. Terrific." Abbie peeled an order blank off the pad while Jack settled the bag by his feet on the other side of the counter.

He first pulled out a five-pound box of chocolates. The delectable scent practically made Abbie swoon.

"My," was all she could manage.

A bottle of cabernet sauvignon followed.

Abbie regarded the expensive label, the foil seal, but said nothing as she put it down on her side of the counter.

When two wine flutes appeared, stems crossed, Jack waggled them between his fingers. She stopped. They were identical to the water glasses she'd purchased for their unfortunate luncheon.

"I liked the style," he said mildly, his gaze colliding with hers. "I've got two more in the bag. But just package these. A pair is far more intimate."

As she took them, Abbie's hand trembled. Her heart lurched, her mind wildly wondering what he meant.

Six varieties of wrapped cheeses, several boxes of gourmet crackers, a salami sausage, a tin of caviar and a ceramic cutting board tumbled onto the counter. Abbie shielded the glasses with both hands as the salami rolled off.

"All this?" she croaked, picking up the salami to point at him.

"Nope. There's more."

"More? But…for heaven's sake, Jack, I'll have to use a laundry basket to get it all in."

Jack chuckled, then winked over his shoulder at the fascinated crowd. "Watch this," he said to no one in particular. "This'll test even Abbie's ingenuity."

A vase, in scintillating lead crystal, claimed the center of the counter. Abbie's eyes widened. The thing was outrageously expensive and probably weighed ten pounds to boot. "Two baskets," she clarified.

Jack grinned, then reached deeper into the bag. He drew out a long florist's box, tied with wide green ribbon.

With her blood thudding through her veins, Abbie fought to be cool, to act every inch the entrepreneur. "I don't do flowers. Perishable. But I'll substitute silk."

He chuckled. "Oh, always out to make a buck, aren't you, Abbie?"

"I can't transport flowers. They'll—"

"Keep them. It's all part of your housewarming—businesswarming?—gift. I wanted to do something special for you today."

Disbelief rolled through her. She accepted the florist's box he handed her as a collective sigh rippled through the onlookers. "Jack. Thank you. I hoped you'd have time to stop, but…this…"

Mrs. Jurgensen stealthily crept away to the punch bowl, where she tapped the ladle against the glass sides. "Anybody need a refill?" she inquired, breaking up the crowd.

"Go ahead. Open it," Jack encouraged when they were alone.

"What did you do?" Abbie paused, willing the moment to last before she edged the ribbon off the corners of the box. She lifted the lid to discover a cache of long-stemmed red roses. Her heart tripped double time.

"One for every day we've been apart."

Abbie's breath lodged in her throat. Somehow she managed to hook a finger beneath the top stem and pull the bud free. "Jack, you shouldn't have. You've been busy. I've been busy. I know that."

"Forget that," he said. "You've been avoiding me."

"No, honestly," she protested. "I've been busy."

"Liar." The accusation rolled off his tongue gently, like an endearment.

Abbie lifted the stem from the box, bringing the bud up to her nose. "Okay. You gave me a lot to think about the other day." She lifted a shoulder. "An old fiancée. The truth about Nat."

"You aren't holding the truth against me, are you?"

"How could I?"

"Okay. Because I've got one more truth for you, then. If you can stand it."

Her eyes lifted.

"I've missed you," he said, his voice barely above a whisper. "I want to see you again. On equal terms, and without Rob—or Natalie—getting in the way. Figured we could celebrate." He tilted his head to the boxes littering the counter. "Crackers and cheese. Fine wine."

She avoided his gaze, testing the rose in the vase. Alone, it drooped forlornly. She remembered what he'd once said about a single rose. "A trial friendship?"

"Uh-uh." She loosened another rose, all of her senses aware of the definite shift in the emotional climate. "I don't think that'll work for us. Can't do friendship, Ab. Not this time."

It took all her resolve to look up at him, to guess what he intended.

"We're too old to get hung up on the past. We've both got a lot of history."

"It isn't the past. It's that you didn't tell me."

"I was wrong," he said simply. "I wanted to forget about Rob. As far as Nat's concerned, after I got here the intents and purposes got mixed up." He lifted both brows. "Kind of lost along the way, if you will."

"If I will," she echoed, feigning annoyance. "If I will."

Jack jumped on the opportunity. "Will you?" he pressed. "Will you share crackers and cheese with me? A few chocolates? Tonight, after your open house?"

She hesitated.

"You want to, Abbie. You know you do."

"I'll be tired...."

One corner of his mouth lifted. "Did I mention I dabble in therapeutic massage?"

She gave up every ounce of resistance. "Is this coercion or persuasion?"

His smile widened. "I know a Swedish technique that'll really loosen up those muscles." His hand trailed over all the goodies he'd brought. "And, the best part of it is, it's part of the package."

Abbie, who, since her open house, had spent a full week putting her new business into overdrive and resuming her friendship with Jack, was bone tired. She cleaned off the dinner table, secretly pleased her father had refused a second helping of dessert and another cup of coffee. He'd put away the leftovers; she'd finish the dishes.

She'd have exactly fifteen minutes to perform a minor miracle with her hair and clothes before Jack arrived.

"You're wearing yourself out, running back and forth with this business, Abbie."

"Starting up's the hard part. It'll slow down."

"We should put a few walls in that upstairs apartment for you. Put in a closet so you can keep a few of your things there. Get it finished in case you want to move in."

"Move in?" She paused, the plate in her hand hovering over the dish drainer. "Where did that come from?"

"You'd save yourself some time. Save Jack a little mileage. He's driving all the way out here to pick you up tonight, isn't he?"

"Yes. But he doesn't mind. And I don't mind, knowing how you hate to eat alone."

Bob Worth snapped the lid on the casserole. "Still. Long hours." He moved last night's leftovers in the fridge to make room for the casserole. "You're seeing a lot of Jack these days."

"His schedule's freeing up a little."

Her father paused to jam the ketchup bottle in the door shelf. "He's been pretty good to you, hasn't he?"

Abbie wrung out the dishrag, then draped it over the faucet. "Very good."

Her father cleared his throat, turning away to reach for a toothpick. "Jack's a good man, Abbie. You should think about that. Girl like you couldn't do much better."

Abbie stared at his back, astonished, before she reminded him, "Jack's only got a few more months before he goes back to the ER."

"So? Nothing keeping you here. Remember that, Boo."

"Daddy! You sound like you're trying to get rid of me!"

"Hey. Life goes on. Things happen. Right?"

"Oh, I don't know. I suppose." She glanced at the wall clock, feigning worry over being late. The conversation was making her uncomfortable. "Look, I've got to run. I have to open early in the morning, so don't worry if you don't see me until dinner tomorrow night."

Her father seemed distracted. "Jack staying?"

"Staying?"

"For dinner tomorrow night?"

"Oh, I don't know. He's always on call, so you have to take him when you can get him."

"Sometimes it's a compromise," he observed, the toothpick waggling from the corner of his mouth.

She didn't answer, her mind on black dress pants and a houndstooth check blouse.

"Boo? Before you go, there's something I want to talk to you about."

She grinned, pausing by the stairs. "What? You aren't giving us your blessing or anything, are you?"

Faint amusement touched her father's leathery cheeks. "Naw," he said, "nothing like that."

Abbie laughed, her father's cryptic words forgotten as she took the steps two at a time. Jack arrived, and the two men were amicably chatting when Abbie, dressed, came back down.

"Shame you had to come all the way out here, Jack, when you two work across the street from each other. I keep telling Abbie I can fix my own dinner. I hate to see you kids bog yourself down running back and forth like this."

"The drive clears my mind," Jack said. "No problem."

Bob Worth looked at his daughter while unconsciously fingering a pearl snap on his Western shirt. "You're lookin' pretty smart for a hurry-up job." He approved.

"Can you believe this man?" she said to Jack. "He's been acting like this all night. Backhanded compliments and unsolicited advice. I think he wants something. Or else he has something up his sleeve."

Jack grinned.

"Well, you haven't exactly been making this easy on me, Abbie. Been trying to find time to talk to you lately." Her father drummed his fingers on the arm of the chair. "I been watching you with all the changes in your life and decided to make a few in mine."

Abbie stilled. "Oh?"

"You won't have to worry about me eating alone much anymore, Boo. That's the thing. Looks like, after all these years, I'll have someone to fix those meals with, someone to share them with."

Abbie's mind fast-forwarded, immediately imagining a girlfriend. It was the only thing that made sense. Her father's recent absences, the nights he retired early claiming he had a letter to write or a call to make. The moments he was preoccupied, distant.

Good God. After all these years, her father had a companion. It was exciting. He'd waited so many years. He deserved so much. This would probably prompt him into the divorce he'd never sought.

"You found someone, Daddy?"

"Yeah. Guess you could say that, Ab. But I like to think I discovered this special woman all over again."

Abbie's heart lurched, relief mingling with fear at the thought of being replaced, of having to share her home with another woman. "Who is she, Daddy?"

"Your mama. She's coming home, Abbie. After all these years, she's finally coming home."

Chapter Eleven

"**S**he's what?" Abigail pulled up short, whirling on him as if she'd been struck broadside. This couldn't be happening. It wasn't possible.

"Your mama's coming home."

"And you're letting her?" she asked incredulously, her voice rising.

"Letting her? Abbie, I suggested it."

"I don't believe this!" Abbie shouted, slamming her purse across the end table. The wooden coasters clattered to the floor. Abbie didn't even give them a second glance. "After she walked out on you? And deserted us? All these years, without a word. Without—"

"Abbie, wait...slow down. You don't understand. She wanted to come home."

"Right. She missed us. That's why she kept those cards and letters coming. And the calls. Why, the phone practically rang off the hook from all her calls."

Her father's worn features were a painful study of restraint. "She couldn't always get to a phone, Abbie."

"Last time I looked, AT&T had hundreds of thousands

of phone lines stretching from one end of the country to the other.''

"Sit down, Boo," her father said wearily, dragging both palms over his temples. "It's time I told you about your mother. And maybe it'll be good to have Jack here with you.''

"Forget it. I'm not listening to this," Abbie shot back, folding her arms across her chest as she dug her heels into the carpet. "Because there's nothing I need to know! I know enough for a lifetime.''

Behind her, Jack moved uncomfortably on the chair.

"Jack?" her father asked. "Maybe with your expertise, maybe you can help Abbie understand what I need to say.''

Abbie whirled, her gaze colliding with Jack's. "What? You already knew about this? Is that why—''

"No," he vehemently denied. "No. First I've heard about it.''

Abbie debated, silently appalled. The situation was humiliating, her behavior infinitely worse. "Okay," she said evenly. "Stay. Please.''

Jack shrugged.

Her father pulled his shoulders off the recliner, then planted his booted feet in front of him and let his hands hang limply between. The suspense became tangible, taunting them, teasing them. "Your mother didn't just run off because she felt like it, Abbie.''

"That's how I remember it," she retorted.

"I suppose so. Because that's how your mother wanted it.''

Abbie stared at her father, unable to comprehend why any woman would want people to think she'd run off and left her family. If there was one hateful bone in Abbie's body, it was directed at her mother, and it had been nourished from her mother's neglect.

"Abbie, it's hard for me to tell you this...."

"Then don't.''

"She was sick, Abbie."

Abbie didn't move, but a tiny tremor of discomfort scuttled under her skin.

"Before she went away your mother made me promise not to tell anyone. And I've kept her secret. I didn't like it, but I did it because that was the way she wanted it."

Abbie drove any hint of a reaction from her features. She was convinced some sordid story was about to jump center stage. Her entire family would look stupid and miserable, making Jack think they were all a bunch of crazies.

God, he'd be scared off for an eternity.

"Your mother was mentally ill, Abbie."

Mentally ill.

She stared at her father.

The two words, though delicately spoken, caused the first brutal fracture in her composure.

Mentally ill.

The words sliced, deadly as a knife.

Disbelief, fear, anger, pooled in her stomach.

"I don't believe it," she said flatly.

"It's true. Sylvie tried to hide it for years. Today the doctors call it bipolar, but back then—"

"No! No, no, no! I don't believe it!" Abbie shouted, her arms shaking from the frustration. "Mother was perfectly sane. She knew exactly what she was doing. Even when she was throwing her temper tantrums and hollering at us and slamming the doors and—"

"She couldn't control her outbursts."

"And the days she'd sleep till noon, not caring how much noise we made, never making meals or—"

"Depression. Triggered by a chemical imbalance in her brain."

Abbie's mouth hung open. It was logical, all of it, yet it went against everything she had grown up believing. "She's conned you. Mother may have been selfish and spoiled, but she was never sick. Never."

"She was so sick we never thought she'd come home again."

"This is stupid! I can't believe you're even considering letting her come home." Abbie snatched her purse off the table and jammed it under her arm. "She's been gone twenty years and now she wants to come back home with a 'poor little me' story so everyone feels sorry for her. I know her game. She's probably broke and down on her luck, and—"

"Abbie, all those years ago, I—I had to institutionalize her."

Abbie was speechless as horrible images floated through her head. Faded, baggy nightgowns that tied in the back. Stark, green-colored walls and long, endless corridors. Patients shrieking and throwing food. Huge rooms with game boards and puzzles and playing cards and a black-and-white TV that was always on.

Abbie's eyes sought out Jack. His expression was grim, his jaw clenched.

"I'm sorry, Abbie. I was wrong to skim a little truth off the top. I shouldn't have let you think she deserted us. But I never thought she'd come home again. Back then, if someone was sick like that—"

The trembling moved from Abbie's arms to her back, her spine. She couldn't control it. It felt like the quaking started from the pit of her stomach and was working its way inside out. "Forget it! I'm not listening, I'm not. I'm going out tonight."

"Abbie," her father chided.

"No! I refuse to postpone another day of my life because of my mother. She's been out of our lives for over twenty years, and I for one am not welcoming her back into mine." Abbie grabbed her coat off the back of the chair and pulled it on, driving one perfectly pressed point of her collar up against her throat. It looked like a Chinese throwing star. She wheeled toward the door, glanced back once at Jack

before crossing the threshold to stomp into the waiting twi-
light.

Jack and Bob Worth both sat silently, unmoving. The
old man's eyes were filled with misery, remorse; the
younger man's with compassion, pity.

"Look. Let me talk to her," Jack said finally. He slowly
levered himself up off the chair and started to leave.

"I never lied to that girl ever before."

Jack paused midstride while Bob Worth absently mas-
saged his arthritic knuckles and stared at the worn carpet.
Intuition told him the old man wasn't looking for a reply,
so Jack reluctantly moved away.

Outside, Abbie hugged the passenger side of his car as
if it was a lifeline. With her hip settled against the door
frame and her back to the house, she stared sightlessly over
the empty acres beyond the barns. Cattle bawled and spar-
rows darted through the dusky skies. She was oblivious to
it all.

Jack touched her shoulder. "You okay?"

"No." She wiped her eyes.

"Mmm. I think your father feels the same."

"He needs to come to his senses. She's using him. She's
probably used him from the beginning."

"Maybe not. What he said in there? Those are classic
symptoms for a bipolar disorder."

"It's too incredible. She deserted us. She's had a job.
She lived in an apartment outside of Minneapolis for years.
Come on." She spread her hands as if willing him to un-
derstand. "Crazy people don't do that."

"People with a bipolar disorder aren't crazy. And they
aren't incapacitated. They're out there, living everyday
lives like everyday people. For some it's worse than others.
She could have had support to live in the community."

Abbie accepted his explanation, then slid frightened,
panicky eyes in his direction. "It could happen to me. It
could—"

He slowly shook his head, his eyelids lowering. "No. There can be a genetic component, but if you haven't exhibited any tendencies..." He let the explanation fade. "Don't concern yourself with that. We're seeing patients who've gone untreated for years who are suddenly leading full lives because of new drugs, new breakthroughs. This is a different age."

Abbie couldn't answer; her cheeks ached from holding back all the reactions clamoring inside her. Her mouth hurt. It was excruciating, this trying not to look like it mattered, trying to look unaffected. All rational thoughts flip-flopped back and forth, making her temples throb.

Part of her wanted to believe the story; the other part adamantly refused.

"If it's true—if it is," she clarified, "then all these years were one big lie. How could he stand by and let it happen? Folks made jokes about it, saying how she jumped the fence and ran off with some other stud. They whispered and laughed, and it was embarrassing. Feeling like trash. Feeling like nobody wanted you, and—"

"It happened that way," he said gently, "because back then, mental illness was a whole lot worse than running off with some stud. There was a stigma attached and no one talked about it, Abbie. It was a deep, dark secret."

"So what you're saying is they locked her up and fed us lies, and it's all okay because—"

"Abbie, stop. I know you're angry. You've every right to be. But she could feel cheated, too. Wouldn't it be strange if, right at this very minute, you were both feeling the same thing? You in South Dakota, she in Minnesota. But you're both seeing the same sky, the same stars. Both scared and a little angry, both wanting to make up for everything you've missed."

"Nice pat answer, but—" she shook her head "—sorry. Too many memories keep crowding in. I did everything I could to please her. She could have tried harder or been a little more tolerant. Maybe she could have toughed it out.''

''It doesn't work that way, Boo. Our physical bodies are governed by hormones. If something's missing or we get shortchanged, it alters our responses. It's like we short-circuit, then act out.''

Abbie pursed her lips, looking like she'd been reprimanded.

''Hey. You don't want a crash course in physiology. I know that. But you should know her behaviors may not have been intentional.''

She tried to straighten, but her bones felt stiff. Jack casually draped an arm over her shoulders, his fingertips brushing the hollow of her shoulder.

''It's a shock,'' he said softly. ''Your coping strategies will kick in.''

''When?'' she asked, her voice strangling as she turned away, blinking back tears. ''I've spent all my life hating her. My own mother! I sacrificed everything to fill in for the horrible hole she left in our lives, and now I find out I didn't even know the real reasons I did it!''

''Abbie.'' He shook her gently. ''Would it have made a difference? Really?''

She sagged against him, spoonlike, feeling helpless and confused and drained. He put both arms around her middle, encircling her. ''I don't know. But there's this part of me that balks at the very idea of having her back. We'd never last two minutes in the same house, not feeling the way I do.''

''Tell me how you feel. Right at this minute.''

''All mixed up and mad as hell.''

He chuckled, his chest vibrating and rumbling against her back. ''Oh. Is that all?''

''Funny.''

''Abbie, you underestimate yourself. You are a remarkably strong woman. Astute, too.'' They clung together, and he rubbed the knobby bones at the top of her spine with his chin. "Have you noticed we'll be late for the movie?"

She snorted, rubbing her nose with the back of her hand. "Who needs a movie? There isn't an action-packed flick that could compare to this bombshell."

Jack chuckled.

For some moments, they swayed together in the growing darkness, engulfed by the night sounds and the cold stinging their cheeks.

"Now it all makes sense," Abbie finally mused. "His preoccupation. The way he wanted my stuff out of the house, the hints about my moving into the upstairs apartment. He wants to move her in and me out."

"Oh, Abbie, I don't think—"

"No. That's it. Now I'm in the way. Can you believe this? He's already thinking what he has to do to keep her happy."

"He may be thinking what he can do to help her adjust."

"I don't think so."

"Abbie, you mean the world to him. He's not going to risk that."

She said nothing, but over his shoulder she watched the moon inch higher over the horizon. So solitary, so alone. So like herself.

"Hey." She sensed a grin as he absently stroked her shoulder with his cheek. "I've got an idea. You could move in with me."

She sniffed, half-amused the small joke could penetrate her melancholy mood. "My, wouldn't that cause a lot of talk?"

"Not if it's completely platonic."

"Right," she said dryly. "We'll hang out a shingle saying completely platonic situation going on here—two roomies sharing old relationship and one new problem."

"Cynical, Abbie. Especially for you."

"Yeah, and you probably want to keep me under observation for clinical reasons. To see what ultimate rejection does to a neurotic woman.''

"Nah. I just want to keep you around. Convince you rejection's just a state of mind.''

Seconds slipped away and into the darkness.

"It isn't, Jack,'' she whispered solemnly. "Rejection gets down in your bones. It second-guesses all your decisions, crippling you while it makes your smile feeble and your fears strong. It puts this little echo in the back of your head, one that keeps reminding you that, no matter what you do, you're just not good enough.''

"That's not true, Abbie,'' he said huskily. "It's simply not true.''

"It is. All these years I tried to prove to myself that I could do whatever my mother should have done, but I could do it better. It became my only purpose. To take care of Meredith and Nat. To make a home for my dad.''

"You did a hell of a job, Abbie.''

"But you know what that little echo in the back of my head kept saying?'' He drew back from her slightly, waiting for the answer. "That I had to do whatever I could to keep things going for Daddy. So he wouldn't leave us, too.''

"Abbie! He wouldn't have, you know that.''

"Try convincing an eight-year-old kid.''

He sighed. "It was traumatic, I know.''

"Can't hold a candle to this. Right now I feel like I've been in slow motion all my life, and it's all been leading up to this grand moment. Unbelievable. She's made a mess of all our lives, and he's welcoming her back with open arms, saying, 'Go ahead, take another crack at it.''' She issued a half laugh, thinking of the lunacy of it. "God, isn't there some saying about how, no matter how you try, you can never go back again?''

He captured her elbow and turned her, stilling her as a moment of silence slipped away. "Don't say that, Abbie,'' he said, turning, suddenly serious as the moonlight silhouetted his profile. "Because I'm trying to do just that. I'd hate to think coming home again was impossible."

Walking back into the house was the hardest thing Abbie had ever done. She had never stormed out before. Never once. Doing so this time left her feeling justified but foolish.

Her father still sat in the same chair, his fingers curled over the armchair covers as he stared at the crack in the far wall. As she moved numbly forward, it occurred to her that she had, only months ago, thought this would be her home forever. Now everything had changed; nothing would wait for her to catch up and make sense of it.

"How long till Mom comes home?"

"Ten more days," he said, his gaze unblinking.

"You know, Daddy, if she was to visit...first...and then..."

"Abigail, your mom and I have lost too much of our lives. She needs to feel like she still has a home. I need to feel like I have a wife."

"I see."

"You know, honey, you probably don't remember it, but she was a great cook. And I want to get her cooking again. I want her to put a few little touches on the house. She always had a way with color. Could toss around a few pillows and make this house look like a mansion. I want her to do those things, and I think if she does, she'll come back into herself."

Abbie couldn't dredge up one logical reply. Instead, she looked around her, to the dismal pieces of furniture her father had always objected to replacing, to the coconut cake he had left untouched on the dining-room table. Suddenly, all her efforts appeared inadequate, second-rate.

"Will she be able to do everything?" she choked out, determined to mask the insecurity in her voice.

"Oh. Absolutely. Don't worry about that. She's looking forward to it."

"Then...then you don't need me around here anymore, do you? Not for the everyday stuff."

"Honey, you're free to do whatever you like. You can throw yourself into the business. Do as you please. Have a little fun."

A horrid, curling sensation struck the center of her chest, then moved lower, to pitch and roll through her stomach. She had to ask the question she dreaded most. "Jack and I were talking, and I got to thinking, maybe I should move into town."

"If that's what you want, go for it. I'd understand."

"Well, I..." The world she'd known, the niche she'd created for herself, came crashing down. She was almost thirty years old and unwanted, unneeded. No one cared whether she came or went. No one even noticed. She was being cast aside, making all the years of self-sacrifice count for nothing. If someone had branded a big, fat zero into her forehead, she couldn't have felt worse. "Then I've decided," she said with far more conviction than she felt, "that that would be best. It's time I moved out."

Chapter Twelve

Abbie packed her things quietly, stoically. She moved her clothes immediately, telling her father not to bother throwing up a few walls in the apartment—she'd call it a loft. But each time she climbed the stairs, the vast open space on the second floor of the building mocked her, exaggerating her despair.

When she took the first batch of her clothes into town, she had to toss them in a corner because she had no closet. All her beautiful new things piled like rags. Hangers tangled together, fabrics twined.

Abbie took a step back, determined to remove herself, to look at the whole picture.

But the whole picture was dismal, deflating.

The walls were bare, the fixtures stark. The single-pane windows, uncovered, at either end of the room offered a bird's-eye glimpse of Cooper, the north and the south ends. The floors were splintered and uneven, with gaping cracks that held decades of dust and dirt. The plaster was cracked and the ceiling had once leaked. It looks like a huge reservoir, she thought, waiting to be filled up with castoffs.

The smoldering lump in her throat grew. She wanted to be strong, she wanted to consider this to be the jumping-off point of her life, but all she could think of was what a horrible mistake her father was making.

Abbie's knees buckled. Folding her legs beneath her, she sank, her bottom meeting the filthy floor as she crouched, her arms clutched around her knees, weeping. Tears burned the backs of her eyelids. To stop them, she jammed both palms against her eyes, but the moisture seeped through, wetting her wrists and sliding down the inside of her arms.

''Oh, God,'' she whispered, everything going blue-black behind her eyes, ''how do I get through this one? How?''

Her life was a mess. She could barely look at her father anymore. For all her growing-up years, he'd fostered the belief in their mother's desertion. He'd sacrificed character and integrity to protect a woman who could be cold and cruel and callous.

In the past thirty-six hours, since finding out about her mother, Abbie's emotions fluctuated between admiration and hatred. Her mother must be courageous to think she could come back and everything would be all right. Either that, or nuts.

Thinking of all the words, all the phrases she'd so recklessly thrown around all these years, she wondered how deeply they'd disturbed her father. The loony bin. Flake. The nuthouse. Crazy old woman. Insane. Nuttier than a fruitcake.

Everything took on new meaning. Everything became more sensitive—including her relationship with Jack.

This morning, she had spoken to him, but the conversation had been filled with awkward pauses. She hung up thinking it would only be a matter of time before he'd detach himself from her and her problems.

Who could blame him? The man was a doctor, not a saint.

* * *

On a soggy wet morning in November, a little over seventy-two hours before her mother was due to arrive in Cooper, Abbie stared at the grime streaking the floor of the stock truck. At the front end, sitting on a tarp, were the mattress and box spring she'd slept on since she was a teenager. Propped against them was the old iron headboard her father had picked up at an auction for two dollars and fifty cents. When she was in high school, she'd painted it orange, lemon and neon green. Today it was a respectable, somewhat quaint, antique gold.

"Here, Abbie. Take this end, will you?" Her father poked a frayed rope through the slatted sides of the truck. "We'll get her tied down so she doesn't shift."

Abbie, with her ungloved hands freezing, slowly reeled in the frayed sisal as if it were lead crystal.

"You sure you don't want to take that pie cupboard down in the basement?"

"No, Dad. That's okay."

"It won't be too much trouble to haul out. I know you're partial to it."

"That's okay."

"It'd be a nice piece to have in your place, and you ain't got much for cupboards."

Abbie glanced at the pitiful assortment she would soon haul into town. A triple dresser that had been repainted three times, a fiberboard wardrobe covered in white laminate, and an occasional chair, upholstered in olive green velvet, the welting threadbare, the tufted buttons missing. Seventeen cornflakes boxes lay scattered over the frosty grass by the back door; they contained all of her worldly possessions.

There was something demeaning, she mused, about having all your valuables transported in cereal boxes. But then, what did it matter? Who would see? The few people who wandered into the doctor's office for their allergy shots? Jack?

Not likely.

She hadn't spoken to him since he'd more or less told her to buck up and hang tough. Easy words for someone who'd made himself remarkably scarce ever since he'd uttered them.

Abbie, working on autopilot, nudged the rope out through the other side of the truck to her father. But she looked up at the distinctive sound of a muffler roaring into the lane.

Jack.

Grinning, he sauntered out of the car, a floppy rain-repellent hat perched jauntily on his head. "Hey, guys," he hollered. "You started without me."

Abbie stepped over to hang her elbows over the slatted sides of the truck. "What're you doing here? I thought Monday mornings were allergy shots."

"I'm flexible," he said, shrugging into an insulated red flannel jacket. "We rearranged all last week's appointments and this week's allergy shots so I could have the day off."

"You didn't." Abbie was aghast, knowing what that must have taken.

"Mmm. And I have an office manager who says you owe her big time."

In the soggy morning light, Abbie's smile was blinding.

Her father never even looked up but instead finished knotting the rope. "Then haul yourself over to that dresser, boy, and give me a hand," he said. "We'll get her in and then bring up that pie cupboard Abbie's always fancied. Kept telling me she didn't want it, but I know better."

Jack pulled the nine empty drawers from the dresser and handed them up to Abbie. She stacked them on end like huge dominoes. Together the men heaved the dresser onto the back of the truck. Jack swung up after it, dragging it to the front to wedge against the mattresses.

"Put the drawers in, Abbie." Her father sniffed, wiping

his nose with the back of his wrist. "I'll clear a path for that pie cupboard. Glad to be shed of it."

After he turned back to the house, Jack and Abbie stood there alone on the bed of the truck. Eight days, and only one phone call had passed between them.

She'd missed him. Desperately. For today, she wanted to hoard every detail that made him special. The way the moisture dripped off the back of his hat to wet his jacket collar. The way the corners of his eyes crinkled and his lips firmed when he'd lifted the dresser onto the truck. The way he moved in jeans and a flannel jacket. His wonderfully exaggerated dimples.

"I wondered what happened to you," she said.

He slid the first two drawers into the dresser before pausing to look over his shoulder at her. "Had to clear my schedule. Had to advise people emergencies were unacceptable on moving day."

"I didn't think you'd come."

He reached for another drawer but, instead of lifting it, toyed with the drawer pull as if it was the most fascinating thing in the world. "Hey, I work like hell to clear my schedule and you doubt me. What kind of friend do you think I am?"

She leaned back against the slats, her arms behind the small of her back. "I don't know. What kind?"

His features relaxed, and he moved slowly, bending over to one-handedly replace the drawer. "The kind who'll always be there for you, Abbie. Don't ever doubt it. Okay?"

Though his reply was sincere, Abbie saw something else: a man who drew a distinct line between friends and lovers. He chose his words carefully, veering far from anything that could be construed as attachment.

"This has been the hardest week of my life," she said. "I wanted to talk to you, but I was afraid to call."

He hunkered down and rocked back on his heels. "I figured some distance would do us both some good. I'm not going to lie to you and say finding out about your mom didn't make me think twice. I came back here to get the complications out of my life, not jump back into them.''

''Then…does it make a difference? Will it?''

He looked at her long and hard, a strange new light behind his eyes. ''Only if we let it,'' he said finally, looking away to snag another drawer.

''But—''

''Boo, let's leave it at that.''

Abbie pulled herself off the slats to hand him the next drawer.

''Thanks.''

They worked silently, but each time their hands held the same drawer, an awareness kicked in. Finally, after putting in the last one, Jack looked at the jumble by the back door.

''You going to have enough room for all your stuff?''

''Too much of it. That apartment's going to be empty.''

He grinned, then jumped off the back of the truck. ''You'll fill it up, Boo. But it won't be because of your stuff. It'll be because of what you put in it.''

Abbie stared after him as he picked up the first cornflakes box. She understood his meaning.

He wasn't giving her hope; neither was he taking it away.

It was bothersome, her being in that sprawling old building across the street. Jack poked a finger between the blinds in his private office to see if her upstairs light was on.

Not yet. Six o'clock. And not a sign of her. Probably working in back. Probably working alone without even a radio for company.

He'd go over and see her if he didn't have all these case files to read. But they couldn't wait. With tomorrow morning set aside for home visits, he had to get the work done now. Tonight, after he got home, after he pulled up the carpet in the small bedroom, he'd call.

He needed to pace himself, plan his time accordingly. Frankly, they needed to pace themselves.

The first page of the file was simple reading, nothing extraordinary. He scanned it, reading quickly.

Nothing registered.

Huh.

Swiveling in his chair again, he flicked his forefinger between the blinds to check. Nope. Nothing. Still dark as a tomb.

Letting the slat fall back into place, his gaze drifted over the report a second time. With pencil in hand, he checked the significant information. Clusters of professional jargon were highlighted. He reread each item; it meant absolutely nothing to him.

Great. Terrific. Hotshot doctor who didn't have a clue. Certainly not about how hormones ruled the adult male body.

Three mind-bending syllables slowly rolled over the tip of his tongue: Abigail.

Dammit! The woman was driving him wild.

He thought about her all the time. Day in, day out. Her timid little smile. Her kisses that could singe the hair off a grown man's chest. The way she laughed. As if her heart was tinkling inside some delicately crafted music box. He found himself saying cutesy things just so he could hear her laugh.

Oh, he was falling for her. Hard. And fast.

He recited every logical argument to prevent his reaction. Like a litany he practiced it. He remembered every womanly wile and every backhanded way women had of gutting a man. God knows, Rob had been a helluva teacher.

On the other hand, Abbie was at the opposite end of the spectrum. She wouldn't intentionally set him up. She'd never be demanding or pouty or difficult.

But this thing between them was getting out of hand.

He'd have to protect her or she'd get hurt. Let her down

gently, that was it. He didn't want to leave with Abbie Worth on his conscience. It wouldn't be right. She was a nice kid. She deserved more. Certainly more than he could give. He'd have to make her see that.

Besides, he hadn't expected this much innocence. He'd thought a fling would be in his best interests. But he couldn't bring himself to push it, not with her. And every time he looked at her, it seemed his hindquarters were on fire.

He groaned, slamming shut the case file.

Oh, what the hell. If he was going to start letting her down, he might as well do it now.

Hauling himself out of the chair, he snapped off the overhead lights, then went out the front way through a waiting room that smelled of old paneling and Lysol. He paused next to the table of dog-eared magazines to make sure the current copy of *Newsweek* was on top. Mr. Jurgensen always stopped by to read it on Wednesday mornings. Strange thing about small-town rituals—he was beginning to appreciate their value.

Outside, two cars were idling in front of the grocery. He recognized both. Huh. Joe Bishop probably needed another carton of cigarettes. Reminding himself to take another shot at extolling the virtues of the nicotine patch, Jack strode across the street.

Once at Abbie's front door, Jack cupped his hand to the glass, hoping to get a glimpse of her. Nothing. Okay, he should have called. He knocked. Nothing. He rapped more loudly, more insistently.

A light flicked on in the back room; Jack strained to see. Abbie's dark silhouette peered around the back wall. Jack dropped back, trying not to look too anxious. He nonchalantly jammed his hands into the back pockets of his jeans, and waited for her to swing open the door.

Abbie, wearing a sweatshirt with the neck cut out of it, anchored her hands on either side of the big brass doorknob. "Hi," she said, leaning a shoulder against the end of the door. "What're you doing?"

"Oh…I…" He shrugged. "Nothing. Just finishing up. Thinking about grabbing a bite to eat."

"Oh." She dragged a hand through her hair, pausing to rub the back of her neck.

Memories of the massage went winging through him. The way she felt beneath his hands, all smooth and firm and pliable. She was different now, removed, distracted.

"I guess it's getting late, isn't it?" She looked up at the sky, at the fading light. "Want me to fix you a sandwich? I stocked the fridge. I've got—"

"No. No, I wasn't looking for a handout, Boo."

"It's no trouble." She opened the door wider.

He shook his head. "You getting along okay?"

"Fine." She shrugged. "As well as can be expected. Tomorrow's the big day. The mama hen comes home to roost."

"Have you got everything ready?"

Abbie snorted and rolled her eyes. "Me? Oh, sure. I cleaned the house, put a pan of lasagna together for her first night home and filled the new car Daddy got her with gas. After that, he asked me to give them a couple of days alone. If he brings me their dirty laundry, I'm drawing the line."

Jack had never heard so much hurt, outrage and bitterness in such a short outburst. Hearing it from Abbie aggravated him.

He touched her arm just above the wrist. "After she's settled, it'll be…" What? Better? He couldn't bring himself to make that prediction. "Easier."

"Great. You're even a bigger optimist than I am."

"How're your sisters taking this?"

"Nat's furious."

"Of course."

"Meredith's willing to give her a chance. I don't know

what's come over the woman. Must be Rowe, and the fact she's expecting their first baby.''

He smiled, thinking of the story she'd told him about Meredith and how she'd remarried her ex after they were named guardians of an orphaned child. "I guess I don't have to ask how you're taking it.''

"As well as can be expected,'' she repeated sourly. "You caught me on the back porch steps with a box cutter.''

His eyes widened in alarm.

She laughed. "Don't worry, Doc. I'm not considering anything serious. Just making paper shred out of seventeen cornflakes boxes. It has a soothing effect.''

"Aw, Abbie...dammit.''

"What? I knew this was going to happen sooner or later. The sooner just got to me, that's all.''

He sighed. "I've got an idea. And it's far better than a box cutter.''

"Let me guess. Intense psychotherapy, followed by sedatives that will put me in a comalike state. That should just about put me in a hospitable frame of mind.''

"No, something less drastic.''

"Don't tell me to hug her and everything will be all right.''

"No. You'll do what's right for you, I'm sure of it.''

She plastered a brave smile on her face. "I wonder what we'll say. Whether we'll shake hands or...or what. Grown kids shake hands with their mothers, don't they?''

"I suppose.''

"I don't relish the idea of getting too close. You've convinced me she isn't contagious or anything, but...'' She raised both shoulders.

He inclined his head, realizing how much he admired her verve. She was gutsy, a comedienne making fun of her own pain. "I want you to close up shop tomorrow morning, Abbie. Take the morning off to be with me.''

"Tomorrow's Friday. I can't."

"Uh-uh. You owe me, Abbie. Big time. I'm making home visits and I want you to come along."

"Why?"

"Because there are some antique shops I've wanted to stop at. Come on. Forget your mother and find some treasure for the loft you claim is eclectic and free-spirited."

She hesitated. "I said free-spirited, Jack, because it's synonymous with decrepit."

"Come with me," he urged. "Let's get out of here. We could spend the night in one of those funky little cabins out at the edge of the reservation."

"The place with the hot tubs?"

"Sure. We could even make it a long weekend. I've got my pager."

"Jack, that's insane." She bit her bottom lip, but her dark eyes debated.

"It's only a couple of days out of your life. I dare you to spend them with me."

"If anybody finds out…"

"Purely respectable. I'll even spring for your own cabin." To his surprise, as well as his regret, that was the deciding argument.

"Okay. Sure. Why not? What have I got to lose except my reputation?"

Chapter Thirteen

As Abbie and Jack headed back to Cooper, the comforting whir of tires made her slump in her seat. "Hey, you. Tired?" Jack's hand inched across the console, lightly stroking each of her knuckles.

"Mmm. Wonderfully so." She sighed, her eyes still closed. "That was a great idea you had. When I get rich, I'm getting a hot tub."

He chuckled, his eyes unashamedly traveling over her breasts, her waist. She'd worn an eye-catching electric blue suit for the hot tub. They'd had the place to themselves the first night and spent two hours spaside, lounging, talking.

"The antique shops were a bust," he said ruefully. "Sorry about that."

"I did like that soda bar, though."

"Twenty-five thou is a bit steep for my kitchen budget."

With her head still on the back of the seat, she turned to grin at him, silently admiring the way he drove. His left hand, wrist bent, hooked over the top of the wheel. His confidence, and the self-assured way his eyes flicked to check the rearview mirror, made her feel safe. Being with him had made her forget.

"The best," she said slowly, "was getting away. Thanks for including me. It really helped. I haven't thought about the mess at home. Not since we left."

His palm covered the back of her hand. "Good."

"I almost hate to end it."

"We can postpone it. I need to stop at home, check the mail."

"Mmm. Do it. I'm in no hurry to get back."

Within five minutes, they were turning the new locks Jack had installed on the back porch. Inside, the phone was ringing.

"Grab that, will you?" he asked, throwing the door open ahead of her. "It's probably the estimate on the sink."

Abbie made a nosedive for the phone. "Hello," she said breathlessly. "Conroy residence."

"And who is this?" a female voice demanded.

Abbie pulled back, blinking. "I…I'm a friend of Jack's. Can I help you?"

"Put him on the phone."

Abbie, growing suspicious, glimpsed the back of Jack's legs as he hurried up the back stairs, loaded down with suitcase, briefcase and a clothes bag. She framed a polite, but obtuse, reply. "Actually, this isn't a good time. Can I take a message? I'd be happy to do so."

Uncertainty hummed over the phone line. "So you're a friend of Jack's, huh? And what, exactly, are you doing there at his place in the middle of the morning?"

Abbie wrapped the phone cord around her wrist, debating. This was Rob, she was sure of it. "I'd rather not say, particularly when I don't know who I'm talking to."

"Rob Stearling. Jack's fiancée."

"Oh. Well." Abbie took a deep breath, refusing to be intimidated. "Hello. I guess that puts a different slant on things. Jack's unpacking his bag right now. We just returned from a weekend, um, getaway.''

The weekend had been perfectly innocent, but Abbie figured Rob didn't need to know that.

''What the—''

''And...Rob? I'm sorry. But about that fiancée thing? That's not the way Jack tells it.''

''Excuse me?''

''He told me all about you. And how long you were together. And why he came back to Cooper because it was over between you.''

''I don't know who the hell you are, but I want to speak to Jack. And I want to do it now!''

Abbie paused, gauging Rob's frustration. ''He doesn't want to speak to you. He wants to move on with his life. See? I was here a few weeks back when he talked you. So I'm trying to be nice here, but—''

''Put him on the phone, you little ninny!''

''Don't make this any more difficult than it needs to be. I'm sure it's not easy, but—''

''I want to talk to him!''

''I'm sorry.''

''What're you doing? Running interference for the man?''

''Rob, listen. Jack doesn't feel the same, not about you. Not anymore. He's done talking. He won't come to the phone.''

''I don't care what he wants!''

Abbie's patience thinned. Now she knew why Jack, after months of being badgered, didn't want to talk about it. ''Listen to yourself, will you? You're embarrassing yourself. You've managed to fix it so you and Jack can't even part as friends.''

''If you think, for one minute, that you're coming between us—''

"I don't have to think that. Because there's nothing left to come between."

"You don't know anything! You don't know how it was between us! You don't—"

"I can only imagine."

"He was with *me* first, before you ever—"

"Rob, whatever you shared with Jack was over and done with before I was ever involved. We're not talking about first come–first served here. So bow out. Gracefully." Abbie punctuated her last words, snapping them off her tongue. "Get over it. Leave him alone."

"It'll never last," Rob predicted. "I give him one more month, and then he'll come running home."

"Maybe, maybe not. But understand this—he wants to go on with his life. And—Rob?—right now he wants to do it with me."

Rob Stearling never said another word before the line went dead.

Abbie sagged against the wall, fearing she'd gone too far. There'd be hell to pay, she was sure of it.

She hung up the phone and looked across the room, straight into Jack's pensive features. The way he stood, poised and framed within the doorway, made her guess he'd heard the last few snippets of conversation.

"That was Rob," she said simply. "I either solved your problem or compounded it."

Three days had passed since the fateful phone call from Rob. In the interim, Jack thought more about Abbie than he'd ever dreamed possible. It amazed him how brutally frank she'd been during the run-in, dubbing her replies classic gut instinct.

He couldn't fault her for it because, whether either of them wanted to admit it or not, he suspected a thread of truth ran through all she'd said.

So Abbie was a territorial creature, he mused, sitting at

his desk after everyone in the office had left, one who re-
acted instinctively, one who had no qualms about marking
her space. One who fought for what, or whom, she wanted.

Equally flattered and concerned, Jack remained convinced he needed to let her go. She didn't have a clue what
it meant to commit your life to being with a physician. She
didn't realize he was still licking his wounds from the fiasco with Rob.

If he had any misgivings about the amount of time they
spent together, he dismissed it, telling himself he was simply proving to Abbie they could be together without any
kissing or hand-holding or side-by-side displays of affection.

But, inside, he balked.

Kissing?

He wanted to desperately.

Hand-holding?

He got away with it by leading her to see something or
checking to see if her hands were too cold. Or too hot.

Or, as in the story about Goldilocks and the three bears,
just right.

Displays of affection?

Forget it. Opening car doors and holding coats were
common courtesies. Pulling her coat zipper up another
notch when the thermometer was hitting forty was prudent,
not affectionate. A pat on the rump when they passed in a
hall or doorway was because, together, they were a tight
squeeze.

Good God. Whom was he trying to kid?

He was in denial. Flat-out denial.

Maybe he should just have an affair with the woman to
get her out of his head. Prove to himself that Abbie and he
were as incompatible as oil and water. One long randy night
with her and he'd be free and clear. He was sure of it. He
should just put his scruples on hold and do it.

Just do it.

Flinging his pen onto the desktop, he yanked the stethoscope from his neck. It had been a long, hard day. He could use a diversion, and Abbie was, after all, a consenting adult.

Instead of going to the front door of Abbie's building, he went to the back. He knocked, then let himself in with the key she had given him.

Clutching a giraffe, Abbie stood surrounded by an outrageous assortment of stuffed animals. Her workroom was cluttered with the fuzzies, every size, shape and color possible.

"Hey. What's up?"

Without much enthusiasm, she waggled the giraffe's head in his direction. "A group from Social Services asked me to put these together for the women's shelter. Most of the women and kids leave without anything but the clothes on their backs."

He studied her as she dispassionately plunged the giraffe into a wide walnut-colored basket. "Depressing work?"

"Yes and no." She looked away, rearranging the stuffed animal among a wealth of toiletries and personal-care items.

"The good part is...?"

"That maybe some child who's alone and a little bit scared will enjoy this guy." She tapped the brown-and-gold giraffe on the snout.

"And the bad part is...?"

"It's given me too much time to wonder what it would be like. To be a woman alone out there. Without your kids. Or your mate."

Or your mate. The phrase, its implications, disturbed him. To Jack, mates were joined on an ethereal level, transcending the flesh and bones of day-to-day living.

"Hitting too close to home?" he asked.

"Maybe."

He watched her, empathy welling inside him. She picked

up a tangerine ribbon, toyed with it, held it up against the giraffe, then brushed it over the wicker-handled basket.

"Have you talked to your mom yet?"

"No. Daddy called, said things were going as well as could be expected." She shrugged and dropped the ribbon back in the box. "He hinted that maybe I should come out. But I...well, I told him I had a lot to do. I mean, there're these baskets, and—"

"And they make a great excuse, don't they?"

She smiled reluctantly. "Yeah. They do."

"Are you afraid? Or just angry?"

"Both. My first reaction was to remind myself she's the same woman, but now, knowing what I know, I've started thinking of her differently. Things are blurring. Nothing's all wrong, nothing's all right."

"Might be a good time to go see her, then, to put it all in perspective and draw a whole new set of conclusions."

"I don't know if I can. Sure, she's my mom, but I don't know her." She wrung her hands, her palms moving up to chafe her wrists. "I don't even know what I'll say. 'Hi, Mom' sounds kind of dumb."

"I don't think she'd notice."

"I suppose I'm going to have to do it eventually."

"Mmm."

"If it goes too long, things get difficult."

He nodded.

"The whole situation makes me feel like I should do something. But I don't know what. Any rules of etiquette for welcoming your mentally ill mother back home?" She looked up at him. "Emily Post ever take a stab at this one?"

He grinned. "Probably not. But I'd guess, from here on out, you make up the protocol."

"Jack?"

"Yeah?"

"Will you go with me?"

"Me?"

"Yeah. For that first time."

He witnessed the vulnerability, the love she had always, only, offered. Nothing ever worked out the way it was supposed to. He'd come over here to extricate himself from an impossible situation, not to dig himself in deeper. Yet one look at her and all resistance evaporated. "Sure, hon. All you need to do is ask."

"Right now? I'm ready to get it over with."

Abbie's old coat hung on a hook by the back door. He pulled it down and held it out to her. "Here. You'll need this. It's getting chilly."

Jack smiled, watching her shrug into it, a silk blouse sliding into quilted canvas. Abigail Worth. His innocent little ragamuffin. An oddball combination of the classic and practical.

She zipped it up, checking her pockets for house keys and gloves.

He couldn't resist. He reached over and pulled up the coat collar snugly, one notch below her earlobes and the wispy ends of her snazzy little haircut. Right up against the graceful arch of her neck.

Yeah, the old, worn-out car coat was just the thing, he reassured himself. She'd feel better, wearing it.

Chapter Fourteen

Abbie's mother and father stood side by side at the sink, washing the dinner dishes.

"Hey, kids, come on in," her father boomed, slapping his tea towel on the back of a chair.

Abbie nodded but couldn't bring herself to look at him. Her gaze kept straying to her mother. Sylvie's hair had grayed to a homey shade of salt-and-pepper, and her eyes, behind stylish, thin-rimmed bifocals, were the color of cocoa.

"Maybe we should have knocked. I…didn't know—"

"Abbie?" her mother said. "Don't be silly. This is still your home." Instead of the strident tone Abbie remembered, her mother's voice was low and well modulated.

They stood there awkwardly—mother and daughter—a room away from each other, staring at the person each had become. One had lost her middle years; the other had lost her youth.

Abbie found her mother, dressed in olive green pants and a matching blouse, to be slender, not thin or middle-aged pudgy. Her complexion was finely lined, delicate. Crow's-feet crimped the corners of her eyes, and smile lines bracketed her trembling mouth.

Her face was full of color, something for which Abbie was unprepared. She expected a dull, washed-out, tired look. But her mother's makeup, from foundation to blusher, was soft shades of a creamy beige. Cranberry lipstick outlined her lips, and her eyebrows, arching above her glasses, were penciled with dark umber. Gold hoops glinted from her earlobes.

This was the woman who was mentally ill? Who had spent half her adult life grappling with the highs and lows of a debilitating bipolar condition?

This woman looked as normal as June Cleaver.

"Come here. Let me see you, dear."

June Cleaver's arms opened. Abbie numbly walked across the room, unable to imagine herself fitting into them.

Her mother, apparently having sensed her discomfiture, stopped, her fingertips ever so slightly wavering beneath Abbie's elbows. "My, my."

"She's as tall as you, Sylvie."

"I guess." Her smile warmed. "And hair just like your mother's."

"So I always thought."

"She takes after your side of the family, Robert."

"Now, now. Got your eyes. Your nose."

Abbie squirmed, feeling like a newborn in a crib.

Her parents didn't notice; they were too busy talking to each other.

She tried looking over her shoulder to catch Jack's eye. But he'd positioned himself unobtrusively in the corner; all she could see was the cuff of his dress shirt, the dark color of his pants. Desperation clawed at her.

The god-awful sense of powerlessness, the same she remembered from the early days after her mother had left, paralyzed her. She didn't want to be this close. She didn't want to feel this way...so helpless and afraid, as if she was offering herself up to be a victim or begging for whatever scrap of attention the woman would throw her way.

She nervously cleared her throat, imperceptibly backing away. "Um, have you met Jack, M-Mo...?" As she stumbled, unable to dredge the appellation from her throat, her mouth opened, then closed. She couldn't say it. She couldn't. "My—my friend, Jack," she lamely amended.

"I—no, but I'd love to, Abigail. Your father tells me he's such a nice young man."

"Jack, I'd like you to meet my..." Horror washed over Abbie. There it was again. Her mother? God forbid, how could she go through this with all the hostility, all the hatred thwacking around her insides.

"Sylvie," her mother smoothly put in, extending her hand to draw Jack into their circle. "Please call me Sylvie. Everyone does."

Jack came forward to shake her hand. "Sylvie it is, then."

Beneath lowered lashes, Abbie surreptitiously noted his reaction. Genuine, as if he accepted the woman just as she was.

"You went to school with my girls."

"I did. But my folks moved to St. Louis after I graduated, so, other than Gramps, I never really had a reason to come back. Not until now."

Her mother moved back, clasping her hands together in front of her. Double rings circled her fourth finger.

Seeing that, and guessing at the implication, provoked Abbie's animosity. "You're wearing your wedding rings," she blurted.

Heads swiveled.

Abbie wanted to shrivel up and die.

"Yes. Do you remember them?" Sylvie held them up for Abbie's inspection. "You always used to play with them. Especially in church. You'd twist them around my finger. Or turn them to make them flash. Remember?"

"Barely." She did, but adamantly refused to admit it.

"Your father said he wanted me wearing them again."

"Oh."

"I was afraid they wouldn't fit."

"I suppose not. Not after all these years."

Her mother dropped her hands, looking properly chastised. But her father sidled in and casually draped his arm over his wife's shoulders. "Figured they'd remind us how we've come full circle, Abbie. I like to think there's times in life it's the little things that help us remember the good stuff."

Too much goodness and light. An abundance of humor and forced happiness. Abbie was drowning in it. Needing a strong dose of reality, she turned on her father. "So why didn't you ever wear yours, Daddy? To remind you?"

"Because," her mother put in quietly, never missing a beat, "I asked him not to take the risk. Too many freak accidents, what with all the machinery he works around. I always said, right from the beginning, I'd wear two for the both of us."

But you didn't, did you? Abbie wanted to shout back at her. *No, you haven't worn them for twenty years and then you come prancing back, showing them off like you're so righteous.*

"Probably a smart move," Jack said. "I've seen some pretty nasty accidents because husbands think they're doing the right thing, keeping a ring on their finger."

Abbie glared at him, wishing he'd never come.

Wishing she'd never come.

The small talk was grating.

All the innuendos, all the incidents of the past, hung in the air, threatening to maim or suffocate the itsy-bitsy reservoir of strength she had left.

Abbie ached to turn into a little kid again; she wanted to scream and kick her feet and demand answers. She was miserable; it was only fair the people around her be miserable, too.

But they stood there looking completely unaffected by the blight that had scarred their lives for twenty years. The whole thing was a joke.

Torn by all the resentment bubbling inside her, Abbie longed to bolt. She looked past Jack to the back door.

Then she saw it.

The snapshots of Meredith and Nat and herself missing from the fridge. The magnets that had once tacked them in place rearranged into a fine, thin line.

Abbie seethed, knowing full well it was the work of her mother. The woman probably couldn't wait to sweep every last reminder of them out the back door. She had probably, secretly, renamed all three of her offspring.

Unwanted. Unimportant. And unacknowledged.

She belligerently fixed her gaze on the refrigerator door. "You took down the pictures."

Silence drifted; people shifted.

"I moved them, Abbie. Over here. Where I could see them." Her mother moved aside, indicating the windowsill above the sink.

Three whimsical ceramic frames, all identical, with corners embellished with red apples, wicker baskets and black-and-white cows. Three poses. Three smiling faces.

Their sixteenth birthdays. Graduation. Meredith's wedding.

The niggling voice that refused to give up and was insulted said, The hypocrisy of it! The nurturing voice that wanted to make amends argued, The sentimentality of it!

Abbie blanched. Everything kept getting mixed up inside. The reasonable and the unreasonable. The voices inside her head that kept arguing over what was wrong, what was right.

"Nice frames. They were my favorite pictures."

Her mother smiled at the photographs. "We should get copies made. So we can all enjoy them."

Abbie lifted a shoulder indifferently. It was heavier, what with the chip on it.

"Hey, Jack," her father cut in, "you ever give free medical advice outside of working hours?"

A premonition went through Abbie, making her pivot. "What's the matter, Daddy? Aren't you feeling well? Have you overdone it with all this commotion?"

"Me? Heavens no, I'm fine. Never better. But I got a yearling out in the barn that got tangled up in barbed wire. I was debating whether to treat him myself or call a vet."

"Jack does people, Daddy, not shorthorns."

"It's okay. I don't mind taking a look."

"Great. Appreciate it."

Her father started for the back door to grab his coat off the hook. Jack followed him and they were gone in an instant, leaving Abbie alone and in the same room with the one person she despised more than anyone in the whole world: her mother.

They studied each other, considering.

"Do you mind if I put these dishes away?"

"No. Go right ahead." Abbie stood uncomfortably in the center of the room, flicking the toe of her shoe over a dried blade of grass on the vinyl.

Her mother turned to the dish drainer. "You know, I thought I used to have an electric skillet around here, but—"

"The heating element burned out and I never replaced it."

"Oh." The baking sheets dropped into place between the narrow shelves Abbie had once rigged up in the lower cupboard. "It's good your father has a lot of patience with me about getting a meal on. It's awful. I can't seem to find a thing in here."

"I guess I rearranged it to suit myself."

Stilted silence followed. Then the blue porcelain roaster rattled into its place.

"Don't we have steak knives, or—"

"Left-hand drawer, clear to the back, beneath the tea towels. I intentionally put them there. So Meredith's little girl, Sophie, wouldn't find them."

"Mmm. Of course." Her mother dropped a spatula into the utensils drawer. "I found a hand mixer, but—"

"The countertop one is downstairs in a box. I always hated it."

Her mother's dark gaze glittered, pinning her. "But I prefer a wire whisk," she finished smoothly. "Is there one?"

"I don't know. If you can't find one, I imagine Daddy'll be happy to run you into town to get one."

"Abbie, I'm perfectly capable of driving myself into town to—"

"Oh, and how is that car running?"

Her mother didn't reply. She walked across the room to the chair where her father had left the tea towel. After whipping it off, she flapped it once, then folded it to drop over the towel bar. "You aren't going to make this easy on me, are you, Abigail?"

"Look, Mother, I'm the mild one of the bunch. Have you talked to Nat or Meredith yet?"

"No...not yet."

"Consider me a practice run."

Her mother's eyebrows lifted, her eyelids dropping. "I see. Well, then, I suppose we should start with—"

"The truth?"

"Okay..." She turned to the sink to stuff the steel-wool pad down the mouth of a ceramic frog. "Abbie, I never thought I'd be home again. I thought, if you believed—"

"What? That having us think you ran out on us because you wanted to would be a lot better?"

"No, that—"

"That if you never wrote or called—not on our birthdays or at Christmas or even at all—that we could learn to live with it?''

"Okay.'' Her mother held up her hand. "Enough. If you want the truth, you're going to give me the courtesy of being able to finish what I need to say because—"

"Finish? I don't think—"

"That's enough, Abigail. I went through plenty of years of therapy so I know at least this much. The rule is I get my say. Uninterrupted. You'll get yours.''

Abbie hesitated. She was being grossly unfair and she knew it.

"Those are the rules. Will you abide by them?''

"Okay. I guess.''

"Come on, then. Let's sit down. Like the adults we've both grown into.'' Her mother pulled out a kitchen chair, offering it to Abbie before taking the one across the table. "What I'd like, Abbie, is for you to give me the time to tell you the things I think you should know. You can think about them. You don't have to answer anything or judge what I say.''

Abbie sniffed.

"Please? Not today.'' Putting her elbows on the table, her mother leaned closer.

Abbie wanted to recoil yet forced herself to sit perfectly still.

"Your father and I always wanted three babies. Only we never thought we'd get them all at once. Those first few years, I was so busy, and it was incredibly wonderful. I felt driven to enjoy it, to cram in as many good memories as I could. But intuition kept reminding me it wasn't going to last. And it didn't, not after you girls got older...."

"No. Are you saying this is our fault? That because of us—"

"Abbie! No.'' Her mother frowned, squaring the place mat beneath her elbow. "My problems started long before you girls were born. When I was in high school, I endured horrendous depressions, but I hid them because my folks accused me of feeling sorry for myself. They humiliated me, telling everyone I was moody and spoiled.''

"Grandma and Grandpa?"

She nodded. "They said there must be something wrong with me to act the way I did. But the way they said it...well...for years, I knew what they meant, so it was best to never let on. But I was dying inside. After I got older, it became too much. I couldn't find a reason to get up in the morning. I couldn't find a reason to keep going. Your father had had enough and insisted I get help. But then, by that time...I was so bad....'' She looked down, unseeing, her fingers unconsciously rolling the wedding rings back and forth. "Hospitalization was the only thing left." She smiled sadly. "The thing is, once you get into a place like that, you can never get out. Somebody's always trying to fix you, always trying to mold you into what they want you to be.''

"You've been on your own for a long time, Mother."

"An apartment in Minneapolis, and a job in a hardware store. But I was always under a doctor's care." She paused. "And I could never reconcile myself to what I'd left behind. It's not easy leaving three kids and a husband."

"Right. You certainly made it look that way."

"No, Abbie. You were always with me. I tried to put you on the back burner. I even made up stories about how terrible my husband was, how difficult my kids were. I fooled my counselors. I fooled my doctors. But I couldn't fool myself.'' She lifted both hands helplessly. "See? I never wanted my kids growing up thinking they had a mother who committed herself, so I made up reasons to stay away.'' She shuddered, her fingers curling into tight fists. "God. What a word. Committed. Like a person's so witless they don't know what's wrong with them."

"Then you knew?"

"Certainly. I knew I was different from everyone else. It wasn't what I wanted, but it happened inside me anyway. But you know what made it worse?" Abbie, caught up in the story, shook her head. "I loved you so much I thought I could spare you the shame. I never once thought I was driving you away. I thought going away and keeping it quiet would be the lesser of two evils."

"How could you think that? Didn't anyone ever say to you how much your kids needed you, how much they missed you?"

"All the time."

"Then...?"

"Abbie, you don't understand. Back when I was growing up, people lived on secrets. They didn't talk about things the way they do now. They whispered about crazy people who went to the insane asylum. I grew up thinking I was one of those people. If it hadn't been for your father..." She darted a look out the window, toward the barns. "Well. Enough said. He's a strong man, Abbie."

"He should've been strong enough to be honest and tell us the truth."

"It had to take a lot of strength to keep the promise I held him to. Consider that my fault. My mistake."

Abbie, blinded by her mother's gentle features and the kindness behind her doe-soft eyes, said, "I don't know that I can ever feel what you want me to."

"I don't know that I can expect you to."

The back door opened, and a lot of stomping echoed on the back porch. Both women smiled at each other, intuitively knowing their men were announcing their arrival. Their time alone was up.

Bob Worth entered first. "He says that calf'll be okay. Just a superficial cut."

Abbie smiled to herself, thinking her father had known that all along. But his ploy had worked. She rose, then walked across the room to the utility drawer. After pulling it open, she reached deep into the back. "Mother," she asked, "is this the whisk you were looking for?"

She extended it like the proverbial olive branch.

Chapter Fifteen

Jack, on the drive over to his house, carefully skirted the subject of Abbie's mother. While there were plenty of opportunities to open up the dialogue, he never pressed her. Abbie was grateful for that.

"Come on in," he invited, throwing open the front door ahead of her. "I want to show you something."

She took a deep breath, appreciating the scent of new paint and varnish. "I love the way this place smells, almost as much as what you've done to it."

"What *we've* done to it," he insisted, snapping on the dining-room lights so she could see the new color. "I'm having the cushion for the window seat reupholstered to match. So you can sit on it."

She glanced at the bare spot, remembering how inviting it looked the first time she'd seen it. That day had been hot, magnetizing. "Mmm, love it." Her fingernail flicked over the wall switch he'd covered. "How are you ever going to leave this place? After all you've put into it."

Jack didn't answer at first, but his eyes pensively roamed the walls before stopping at the brass chandelier. "I've wondered that myself," he confided. "Kind of hurts a little, thinking another family could change everything we've done."

His confession warmed her. She longed to tell him he didn't have to move back to Omaha, but she couldn't bring herself to say it. Her emotions were already strained.

"I can't imagine anyone else living here," she finally said. "But you haven't much time left. Will you leave by Christmas?"

"Probably."

"I'll never drive by this house again without seeing your signature on it."

Jack carefully nudged aside a can of paint, pushing it inside the doorway. "You know what's wrong with all this work? Gives you too much thinking time."

"I know. I felt the same when I worked on the loft. You start second-guessing everything."

"No kidding. It's making me wonder why I even want to go back to Omaha."

She pivoted on the heel of her shoe, hope burgeoning in the area of her heart. "Jack—"

"No," he said firmly, as if he hadn't even heard her, as if he wasn't even aware he'd interrupted her. "There's no choice. This is a temporary situation. I knew that from the beginning. In fact, I wanted it that way."

"People change, Jack."

He looked her way, his eyes lighting on her hair, her mouth. "Yeah. They sure do."

"Jack, I meant—"

"Look," he said, shaking his head as if he was flinging aside any foolish notions, "I promised myself we wouldn't get bogged down. Not tonight. But I did want you to see this...." He stepped to the dining-room table, to the stack of mail piled on the corner. "Look at this. What do you see?"

He fanned the envelopes in front of her nose.

"Bills. What else?"

He chuckled. "Come here. Let me show you another thing." Pitching the mail aside, he led her through the foyer and into the kitchen to stop in front of the answering machine. "Check this out."

"What?"

"No calls."

"So?"

"No calls. No letters. Not from Rob. I think you're the one who made the difference, m'dear."

She wiggled her hand free, protesting. "Jack, I don't think I'm the one who—"

"You are. Eklund said she called him and told him that I, the dastardly doctor of deviltry, had proved unfaithful."

Abbie's jaw dropped. "What? Why, I never said that—"

He chuckled. "I don't care what you said. But I'm impressed with the way you handle people."

"Right."

He tossed a playful arm around her shoulders, pulling her against him and nuzzling her temple before whispering, "And me. I'm impressed with the way you handle *me*."

A foolish thrill wiggled into her stomach. "Oh, Jack, I didn't do anything special."

"Huh. I'm convinced that every day you spend in this world, you do something special." He paused, a teasing light in his eyes. "So listen. Cooper's annual barn dance is coming up. I've been keeping that night open, thinking you'd do the Sadie Hawkins thing and ask me." She looked up at him, genuinely surprised. He poked her in the ribs. "You aren't, are you?"

"Well, I—I hadn't even thought of it, not with all the stuff at home, and...and you're usually on call, and..." she trailed off, leaving the rest unsaid.

"Okay. So *I'm* asking you. Is it a date? Next Friday night?"

"Let me get this straight. You want to jump out of the frying pan with Rob and into the fire with me?"

His enthusiasm fizzled. His expression went from solemn to thoughtful. Then his dimples disappeared. He wound his forefinger through a wispy length of hair near her ear. "Maybe."

"Maybe? You think I'm the kind of girl who'll settle for maybe?"

"Maybe you will and maybe you won't."

Abbie heard the innuendo in his singsong reply. She shivered, wondering how a man and woman went from platonic to erotic. If there was a how-to plan, she'd pay dearly for it. "Does it make a difference," she asked slowly, "whether I will or whether I won't?"

He chuckled, his back arching before the back of his head thunked against the wall. He pulled her closer. "Watch it," he warned. "That fire you mentioned? You're playing with it. And it's a dangerous commodity, Abbie. Especially where I'm concerned."

"Tell me," she said earnestly, wanting to please him. "Tell me what you mean."

His gaze glittered, his smile tight. "If there's one thing about you I love, Abbie, it's also the thing I wish I could change." He hesitated, then added, "Your innocence, Abbie. You'll always be too damned innocent for a man like me."

Abbie woke up the following morning feeling like a different person. Life was beginning to look up. Her mother wasn't the mad housewife she'd once imagined. Jack had actually used her name and love in the same sentence.

Like the poets said, there must be a God.

The affirmations she once employed to help herself feel better changed. Now she told herself that, aside from developing a healthy relationship with her mother, she could be the woman, the lover, Jack needed in his life.

To her, the equation was simple: if she wanted Jack Conroy, she had to pursue him and skip the niceties.

The phrase ''sex, lies and videotapes'' popped into her head, taunting her.

That settled it. She would willingly put anything on the line. Including the innocence Jack claimed he was so fond of.

The barn dance, with Christmas lights strung from the barn rafters and hay bales propped against the walls for seats, was the fall social event. Dress was casual; most wore jeans and T-shirts. Trestle tables at the back of the barn offered up a dozen different kinds of pie and loose-meat sandwiches. The scent of coffee mingled with the dusty smell of grain.

The local auctioneer, Ray Perkins, grasped the neck of his fiddle and let the rib side slide down his thigh as he stepped up to the microphone. ''Consider this fair warning,'' he said, his mellow voice oozing over the speakers. ''We had a request, so it's gonna get mushy out on that dance floor. An' we're movin' along from country swing. Just to show we can.''

Immediately, two measured beats passed before the music hit a shattering crescendo.

When a man loves a woman...

Jack opened his arms; Abbie drifted into them.

Someone threw the lights, putting the dance floor in darkness as hundreds of twinkle lights glimmered.

''Oh, my,'' Abbie murmured, twining her arms around Jack's neck. The illusion was perfect. A dark, warm night, a million stars overhead.

Jack moved closer, whispering against her ear, ''Reminds me of our last prom. Remember? That little footbridge, the fake cherry blossoms and the twinkle lights?''

Abbie stalled, imperceptibly pulling back. ''Actually...no. I didn't go.''

"Oh. I—I'm sorry."

An awkward silence shuffled between them.

Abbie moved back in, closer than before. "It doesn't matter that you mentioned it. So don't apologize. Things like that don't matter to me."

"They should, Abbie."

"What?"

"How stupid we all were. Eighteen-year-old boys who couldn't see the roses for the thorns." His palm smoothly moved up her spine to rest possessively between her shoulder blades. "If I had it to do over again, I would, Abbie."

"Jack, don't. Please. You don't have to explain how you felt ten years ago."

"Even so—" he leaned into her, brushing a kiss over her temple "—I regret my mistake."

Heady anticipation, while the pulsing beat of the music, of guitars, of keyboards and drums, rushed over them. They swayed. Their thighs brushed, and her legs intertwined with his. For one stanza they claimed the darkest corner of the dance floor.

"Jack?"

"Mmm?" The response was more like a groan.

"Can we leave early?"

He lifted his head from hers. Even in the darkness, she could see his eyes were needy. Suggestion hummed between them.

It was Abbie who broke the silence. "Um, this talk show I was watching?"

He stared at her, his eyebrows lifting.

"They said most men like soft, feminine things in a woman's bedroom. Boudoir, they called it. They said men like being invited into a woman's *boudoir*," she emphasized. "Tell me. Do you think that's true, Jack?"

His mouth opened and closed. He said nothing.

"I need to know, Jack."

"I—I don't know...not exactly...."

"Jack?"

"Mmm?" Again, that pained noise.

"I finished decorating my bedroom. There's a new down comforter and pillow shams and, well...I suppose I shouldn't admit it, but I splurged on satin sheets. Expensive ones. They're black and pink...and very, very sexy," she drawled, her fingertips wandering down over his shirt collar to play with the button at the neck before lifting to trace the curve of his jaw. "Black sheets. I don't know what made me do that."

"Can't imagine," he replied hoarsely.

"So anyway, I got to thinking...I've spent the past few weeks checking out your progress with the house, so I wondered if you wanted to check out mine?"

He groaned, and his eyelids went half-mast. "A herd of wild horses or anything as mundane as logic and common sense couldn't keep me away."

He grabbed her hand and together they ducked out the back door, going by the hedgerow. Their path would lead them past dozens of parked cars and onto Main Street. When someone called out, Jack crouched behind a truck, pulling Abbie down with him. They giggled, bent over double as they clung to the bumper.

"Damn. I thought that was for me. This is not a night to be sidetracked."

"You're avoiding people?"

"Honey, tonight I'm spending the evening with you."

They ran the last four blocks to her house, avoiding the streetlamps and snatching breathless kisses on the corners. They giddily skipped up her back porch steps.

She slid the key into the lock. He turned the knob.

With the door half-open, he swooped down, his lips over hers. They stumbled inside, all clutching arms and legs that twisted around the door until Abbie's shoulder blades were pinned to the back of it. The lock clicked, and his full weight was pressed upon her.

"God, Abbie, I want you," he muttered thickly, yanking the hem of her new blouse from inside the waist of her jeans.

His fingers stroked the soft flesh of her belly, the convex arch of her rib. The sensations were exquisite, making Abbie vaguely wonder if it was possible to die from sheer ecstasy. She pulled her mouth free to slather kisses upon his cheek, his earlobe, his neck.

Her hands rode the flat welt seam at the back of his jeans before exploring the rivets on the back pockets, the leather belt threading through the belt loops. She gave a little tug.

Jack shuddered. But his palm inched upward to the elastic shirring of her bra. His fingers curved beneath her arm while his thumb stroked the underside of her breast.

She resisted, her upper arms clenching tight against her body. "No. C'mon, Conroy, I'm trying to get you upstairs. To show you something."

"You're showing me something all right. About how damned perfect you are...." He claimed her breast, cupping it, letting the nipple settle into his palm before rubbing the first of all four knuckles over the tip.

Abbie arched, her spine lifting off the steel door, her breasts thrusting into him, into his hand, his chest. "Jack, I..." She broke off, her voice faltering before a whimper tore through her throat.

He burrowed into the soft spot where her neck and shoulder joined. "Abbie?" His voice was muffled, his mouth warm and moist against her flesh. "Boo baby, if I stay...I don't want to regret what comes next. You sure this is what you want?"

"Stay," she implored. "Stay."

He lifted the long, lean length of her, folding her into his arms to carry her up the narrow, uneven stairs.

Shimmering phosphorescence from the alley vapor lamp glowed through the back window, sending a beam across the farthest part of the room, stippling her new comforter and her old repainted bed. The sheets were turned down. In a moment of whimsy she'd strewn rose petals across the pillowcases. The potpourri—aptly named Heavenscent—had been sprinkled in a huge glass bowl next to the bed.

"Wait," she instructed. "Over there, to the bookcase."

He waltzed two steps to the side, swinging her in his arms.

In the dark, Abbie groped for the Play button on her new CD system, the one Meredith and Rowe had sent as a housewarming gift. She found it, punched it. Easy-listening background music filtered through the speakers.

He laughed, the sound low and throaty, as he headed for the bed. "My, my. Setting the stage, are we?"

"I just want everything right."

"Nothing wrong with that, Boo."

"No. I guess not. Not for the first time."

His stride broke, the easy fluidity of moments before disappearing. "Abbie, I—"

Deep-seated fear washed over her. She couldn't lose him now. Not now. Not when this was all she had.

Hooking her forearm around the back of his neck, she forced his head down. As their mouths met, she clung to him, her tongue laving intimately inside and behind his lips.

The muscles in his neck, his arms, his shoulders, forgot their purpose. He relaxed. He responded.

Abbie relinquished the kiss, submitting to Jack and consciously letting him take the lead. She never willed her own sensual response. It simply happened.

They writhed there, she in his arms, suspended over her bed, fulfillment mere moments away.

Abruptly, he pulled free. "Dammit, Abbie, if you've never...then—then how'd you learn to do that!"

She smoothed the hair at his temple, tunneling her fingers through his hair. "From you."

An expletive tore from his mouth.

"I may be a late bloomer, but I'm a fast learner, Conroy." To accentuate her claim, she undid the top button on his shirt, skimming her fingertips over his chest before dropping down to the next one. "And I'm very impatient to work with."

The sultry heat in her voice was intoxicating.

"Dammit, woman, you're driving me wild," he rasped. "I've traveled all over the country—and never have I met a woman who intrigues me like you. Not one." He lowered her to the bed, placing her across the width of it.

She pushed the comforter back and out of the way to make room for him.

His knee was on the bed, depressing the mattress at her hips, beneath her buttocks, when the telephone beside the bed jangled.

Both of them started.

"Oh, God."

"I'm not here," he said huskily.

"If it's an emergency?"

"Take a message."

She hesitated, fighting to control her breathing, her shaking fingers. Snagging the phone, she dragged it over the sheets and up beneath her chin. She cleared her throat. "Hello?"

"Abbie?"

She shifted, sitting straighter, guiltily, as if she'd been caught. "Dad?"

"Honey, I've been calling all night. Where've you been?"

"The barn dance. We just got in. I mean, I—I just got in." She swallowed, wondering how foolish she sounded. "So, um, what's up?"

Jack laughed right out loud. Abbie covered the mouthpiece.

"Is your mother with you?"

"Mom? No..."

"She's not..." Her father emitted an anguished, bestial

sound. Abbie's flesh went clammy, goose bumps popping out on her arms. "She's gone, Abbie."

"Daddy? What do you mean, she's gone?"

"She took the car and...I don't know. She had a hair appointment, but that was over eight hours ago. I've called all over. Something must've happened to her."

"All right. Hold on, Daddy, Jack and I'll be right out," she said, lifting herself off the mattress and past Jack's hunched frame. She tossed the receiver back onto the cradle, then stuffed the hem of her shirt back in the waistband of her jeans.

"Your mother," he said.

"She's gone!" Abbie dropped to the floor, searching for her lost skimmers. "I can't believe she just ran off like that!"

"Maybe she needed some time away. To adjust."

"Adjust?" Abbie looked over her shoulder to Jack's silhouette. "Don't kid yourself. She ran off. Daddy's beside himself. I've never heard him sound like that before."

He sighed, then reached over to turn on the bedside lamp Abbie had conscientiously put a fifteen-watt bulb in last night. "She hasn't quit taking her medicine, has she?"

Abbie shrugged, sitting cross-legged on the floor to pull on the first shoe.

"Not taking it could alter her behavior."

She sat there, with one shoe on, considering. "You know what I think? She couldn't handle it. Same song, second verse. Things aren't working out, so she runs away. But maybe this time it'll be for good."

Chapter Sixteen

At three in the morning, Abbie called the sheriff, then she called her sisters.

Meredith was disappointed, not surprised. "I was afraid it'd never work," she said. "Not after all these years."

But Natalie's response gave her a jolt. "That's it!" she huffed. "I'm coming back. You aren't going through this alone. Not again."

"Natalie, it could be nothing. Mother could turn up in a couple of hours with some reasonable explanation."

"Get a grip, Ab. It's our fly-by-night mother you're talking about."

"You can't just take off. What about your job?"

"They owe me overtime. This'll call it even."

"But Carl? What'll he say?"

"Who?"

"Carl. The guy you've been ranting and raving about."

"Oh. Him."

"Well?"

"Abbie...there's something I've been meaning to tell you...." An uneasy premonition scurried through Abbie's brain. "You know how you and Meredith are always after me to get a real boyfriend and get past my man-of-the-month fascination?"

Abbie held her breath. "Yes?"

"Well, I did. Sort of. Everything's been going so well since I moved to Rapid City, I thought, shoot, why not give the folks at home the whole enchilada? Let 'em rest easy for a change. I've given them enough worries. So, Carl, he's a real character. A flight of fancy. Kind of a figment of my imagination, if you will."

"But you said Carl was about to propose! You two were this close—this close!—to getting married!"

"I made him up, Abbie."

"You what?"

"So don't worry about me leaving him behind. Trust me, he doesn't care. He wants me to be there with you."

It took a moment for the truth to sink in. "Good God, Natalie. You're as nutty as Mother."

Natalie roared. "Ha! That was a low blow, Ab."

"For all these months, you intentionally let us believe that you and this—this Carl, were going to—"

"Abbie. Get over it. Carl was a little white lie that plucked one more worry from your brain. So what? Consider this my confession and be merciful, will you?"

Through Abbie's astonishment, the deep-seated fear she had doggedly tried to push away finally surfaced. Jack and Natalie would see each other again. She looked across the room to where Jack, head bent, looked over her mother's prescriptions, calculating how much was missing from each bottle. Without saying it, she knew he feared she'd taken an overdose.

There was no way out of this.

"Natalie," she said wearily, "I have a confession to make, too. But it can wait until you get home."

Abbie hung up, convinced the precious time she had left with Jack was about to be cut short. There was only one thing to do. Tackle it head-on and stand up for the thing she wanted most in the world: Jack Conroy.

When the first fingers of a pale dawn inched into the Worth kitchen, the three of them—Abbie, Jack and her father—silently hunched around the kitchen table, lacing their fingers around mugs of coffee. Through bleary eyes, they watched as the steam rose and unfurled. No one drank a drop, but it was good for hand-holding. For warmth and comfort.

None of them had slept a wink. Hadn't even tried.

The sheriff had stopped by, reluctant to search for Sylvie. Given her history, he'd said, it was more than likely she run off because she'd wanted to. But they'd keep an eye out for her, he promised. And they'd keep it quiet.

Out of respect for the family.

Abbie surreptitiously glanced at her father while the sheriff went through his spiel, witnessing how humiliation could honestly beat a man down. All the years of silence. For this.

Later, at the sheriff's suggestion, the men searched the barns and outbuildings. They all imagined the worst. Abbie went through her mother's things, looking for any clue that something—anything—was missing. She came up empty-handed.

They called the hospital and her mother's doctors in Minneapolis. No one had heard from Sylvie.

Then they waited.

They waited for the phone to ring. They waited for the sheriff's car to turn into the driveway. They waited for Natalie.

Long stretches of silence mingled with worried conjecture about where her mother could be, what could have happened. The possibilities were ominous, staggering; the wait-and-see process exhausting.

It was 7:00 a.m. when Jack pushed back from the table.

"Maybe we should go out and look," he suggested. "You've called everyone you know, Bob. Maybe getting up and moving around might help. At least make us feel like we're doing something."

Her father's features remained grim. "Someone's got to stay here in case she comes back. And I've got cows to feed. Even with Sylvie missing, the work's got to be done."

Abbie sat back, imagining how, as a rancher, he'd had to put everything on the line time and again. "This must be just like before, huh, Daddy?"

"No, not like before." Her father heaved a sigh. "A whole lot easier taking care of a bunch of cows today than three little girls twenty years ago."

"But you did a good job of it, Daddy."

"I don't know. I was younger then. I did what I had to do." He tapped the handle of the mug, reflectively turning it in quarter rotations. "Looks like, this time around, I botched it with your mother, didn't I?"

"Maybe not. But if she never comes back, for whatever reason, you'll always have us. Always."

For a moment, he didn't say a word, just moved his mug to another spot, then finger ironed the ring the ceramic bottom had made in the tablecloth. "Funny thing about kids, Abbie. You have them and they're yours, but you're always letting them go." Tears welled in his eyes; he made no attempt to hide them. "Hardest thing ever, lettin' my three little bright spots go. I knew it was coming. Meredith and Rowe getting back together. Then Natalie moving off. You and this business of yours. And you, Jack—" he lifted a brow in Jack's direction "—coming into my baby's life like that. Maybe that's why I wanted Sylvie back so bad. I needed that woman to fill up all I was giving away."

Abbie blinked, her eyes stinging. Her nose went stuffy, and she reached for a box of tissues.

"I see you moving on with your life," her father went on, "and a corner of my heart breaks for all I have to put behind in mine. One of these days you'll be an old married woman, Abbie, with babies who'll make me a grandpa.'' He smiled at her, his eyes warming for the first time in hours. "Hate the thought of giving you away, though.''

For several moments, a poignant nonthreatening silence bound them.

"Come on,'' Jack said finally, standing. "Let's get out of here and feed those old cows you're so fond of. And don't worry about Abbie,'' he said, winking. "Or me. She's too stubborn to ever leave you, and I'm too kind to take her away.''

After the men went to the barns, Abbie wandered around the kitchen, thinking about Jack's cryptic admission. In the height of all this mess, she couldn't believe he said he wouldn't marry her. At least that's what he meant, she was sure of it.

Abbie fixed her gaze on the phone, willing it to ring. Nothing.

She took it off the hook to make sure it was working.

Anger and worry over her mother's fate melded. Doubt and worry over her relationship with Jack multiplied.

A car whirled into the drive, and Abbie ran to the window in time to see the back tires spew up gravel. Natalie. Like always, on two wheels.

Abbie went out on the porch without bothering with a coat.

"Heard anything?'' Nat hollered, clambering out of the car, then snatching her overnight case from the back seat.

"Not a thing.'' Abbie moved toward her, accepting Nat's hug before she took the suitcase from her. "But can we talk about Mother later? Come in,'' she said, moving ahead of her. "You need to know something else.''

"Forget the confession. I already know.''

"You—you do?'' Abbie stopped short, poised on the top

step, holding the screen door for her sister, taking in her wild new perm, her designer jeans and leather jacket.

"Sure. Daddy told me all about the tantrum you threw over Mother coming home. No big deal. You're entitled." Nat took her arm just above the elbow to give her an emphatic shake. "You certainly didn't drive her away if that's what you're thinking. Get that out of your head."

"That's not what I'm thinking." Abbie waited for her sister to step inside, then followed her.

"I'm telling you, if it had been me, I'd have worn my big black hat and headed her off at the pass while I wielded a one-way ticket back to where she came from."

Abbie snorted. "It isn't that, Nat."

"Then what? You think the old witch got a new boyfriend and cleared Daddy's bank account?"

"That possibility hadn't even entered my mind."

"Okay. Something worse?"

"Maybe," Abbie said slowly as they moved into the kitchen. "For you." Natalie stared at her, her brow furrowing as she peeled off her jacket. "This may be a shock, but you have to know. It can't wait. Not any longer." She drew a long, deep breath, then dropped Nat's suitcase next to the open spot near the fridge, wishing she could organize her rattled thoughts. "Jack Conroy's here. At the ranch."

"Jack? You're kidding."

"He's been back in town for several months. Filling in for Doc Winston."

"I'll be damned. Daddy never mentioned it. The rat."

Abbie hesitated, then deliberately reached for a glass. After her long drive, Nat would crave a little caffeine and she always chose soda over coffee. "That's because I asked him not to, Nat."

"What? Why?"

"Because I didn't know how you'd feel about it."

"Why would I care?"

Abbie filled the glass and handed it over. "Because

we're dating—well, no," she revised after glimpsing Nat's startled expression, "seeing each other."

The soda spilled over the rim and dribbled onto the floor.

"I didn't know how to tell you because I didn't want to hurt you." Natalie's features crumpled, her dark eyes confused. "But—see?—Jack and I just keep getting closer. We feel a lot for each other. And, I'm sorry, but we enjoy being together."

"Abbie! Will you stop? Just stop a minute and tell me what's so damn wrong with this picture?"

"Well, I know you two went together in high school—"

"So?"

"So I don't want you to think we intentionally—"

"Abbie, get a life. That was over ten years ago. Before French-kissing and groping in the dark."

Abbie's face flamed. "I—we, well, that wasn't what I..."

Natalie collapsed into the nearest chair, burying her face in her hands, her shoulders convulsing. Abbie stared at Nat, unsure whether she was laughing or crying.

When Nat raised her head, her eyes were watering, her mouth twitching. "I wasn't asking, Abbie. I don't even care."

"But—"

"Abbie, I came home because of this mess with Mother. Jack's a wonderful guy. I'm glad you found each other. But don't worry about me. Or how I feel. Right now, you need to take care of yourself because you're the one keeping the family together. Put your energies into that and forget all this drivel about old romances and high school sweethearts."

Two hours after Abbie put on supper—which the others only picked at—the county sheriff pulled into the Worth driveway.

"Got something for you," he said, hitching up his pants

as he climbed out of his vehicle. "Found the car out past the highway. Overturned and in that ditch out by the McCallister place. Looks like she rolled it." Bob Worth's face drained, making him look older, grayer. "Kind of an out-of-the-way spot, and no one saw it till about an hour ago. I got deputies pokin' around. Hell of it is, it looks like an accident. Her coat's still in the car. But Sylvie's nowhere to be found. Can't figure if somebody picked her up or what."

Bob Worth's shoulders collapsed, his robust chest caving in as if he'd been hit with a shell. "How bad was it?"

"Car's totaled."

Abbie stepped in, her willowy body moving to shield her father. "Should we call a wrecker, or wait?"

"Wait. I want to make sure we don't miss nothin'."

"Fine." Abbie took her father's arm. "Come on. We can make a few calls. We know all the folks around that area."

Jack shook the sheriff's hand. "Thanks, we appreciate it," he said. "You learn anything else, give us a call."

Then he helped get Bob into the house. Back in the kitchen, he slid a chair under him, automatically lifting the older man's wrist to feel for his pulse.

"Reckon we ought to get out there," Bob said.

"Let's see what the cops find first," Jack said smoothly, falling into his professional tone. "How you feeling about this?"

"Got my worries," the older man admitted.

"It was probably an accident, nothing more," Abbie put in gently. "They'll find her at a hospital and—"

"And what if she rolled that car on purpose? We had a few words before she left for the hairdresser's. I didn't think nothing of it myself," he said. "But—"

"No, she wouldn't," Abbie said firmly. "Here." She slipped a glass of orange juice and two aspirins next to his elbow. "Take these."

"I could get you something stronger, Bob," Jack offered.

"Nah, nah, I'll be fine." He flapped his hand in their direction before scooping up the tablets.

"Why don't you get some rest, Daddy? You haven't slept all night. Maybe by then we'll know something."

"I ought to go out there."

"To do what?"

"I don't know. Make myself useful."

"The most useful thing you can do," Jack said, "is stay here and be here when they find her."

"Maybe." Her father grunted from the effort of trying to stand, the joints in his knees popping for good measure. He shuffled over to the stairwell. "Call me if you hear."

"We will," Abbie assured him. Bone tired, she reached for the phone book. "Let's call the neighbors bordering the McCallisters," she said to Nat.

"Go ahead," Nat said, propping her feet on a chair.

Sighing, Abbie grabbed a pencil. Then she stopped short. "Can't do it," she said simply. "This time, I need some help."

Natalie stared at her, dumbfounded.

"Your sister's been up all night," Jack intervened. "I think she'd appreciate someone sharing the load."

A dawning light flickered behind Nat's dark eyes as she pulled her feet off the chair. "Wake-up call," she said softly. "I said I'd come back to help, but I'm still letting you take care of us, Abbie. I promise that's going to change."

It took the three of them forty-seven minutes to confirm what the sheriff's department already knew. No one had seen hide nor hair of their mother.

They caught snatches of sleep through that night and into the next morning. By the afternoon, everyone was short-tempered and grasping at straws.

"Betcha she plotted it."

"Natalie!"

Nat lifted both hands. "I don't trust the woman!"

"Oh, I don't know what to think anymore!" Abbie pitched a pot holder across the table, not caring where it landed. "I hate this waiting! I hate it! It's just like before. Thinking she'll be back. Thinking there's something we can do!"

"There is," Jack said, grasping her fingertips to pull her closer. "Sit down." He pulled her toward his lap, but Abbie veered away, worried what Nat would think. Finally, realizing she didn't even care, that she needed Jack's comforting touch, she sank onto his knees. "Have you heard the phrase 'No news is good news'?" he asked.

"Jack, no. I've spent all these past few weeks trying to make myself believe I must have been wrong. But I'm beginning to think she's suckered us a second time." Her head dropped forward, her forehead rolling against the warm spot on his neck. His hand wandered up her spine to massage her back.

She hadn't felt this loved for years and years. Any embarrassment at being observed by her sister faded.

Let her know, she thought. *Let her know how very, very much I love this man.*

The phone rang, jarring her.

"I'll get it," Natalie said, striding across the room. "Yes? Um, just a minute. Abbie? It's for you. Or Jack."

Abbie reluctantly pulled herself up to take the phone. "Hello?"

"Abigail? This is Rob Stearling. We spoke a few days ago."

Abbie went brittle. "How did you get this number?"

"From Jack's office manager. I said it was an emergency."

"Then dial 9-1-1." Abbie's flip answer earned her dead silence. "Don't bother us again," she went on, "because we don't do repeat phone consultations."

"What?"

"You didn't get it the first time. *I'm* the woman in his life now," she said forcefully, her eyes locking with Jack's, "and I plan to stay there for as long as he'll have me."

"Well, I—I just called to say you're welcome to him. I'm going on with my life," she sniffed.

"Good. I'm doing the same. And—Rob?—if it's any consolation," she added on a gentler note, "I appreciate how difficult that can be."

Abbie hung up the phone. Jack stood, never taking his eyes off her. His look was dark, smoldering.

"Come on," he said, snagging her arm. "I'm getting you out of here. You need a change of scenery."

Chapter Seventeen

Jack and Abbie, with the tension escalating between them, silently slid into his car. They were a mile from the ranch when Abbie screwed up her courage to say what was on her mind.

"You're angry with me."

His foot experimentally touched the brake before his head swiveled in her direction. "No. Why would I be?"

"I shouldn't have said that. About being the only woman in your life."

He looked back at the road, focusing on the upcoming intersection. "We could turn here," he suggested. "The accident site can't be more than five, six miles away."

Abbie, realizing her question had never been answered, nodded stiffly. "Do that. I need to see for myself. Maybe it will make this all seem more real." She stared out the side window. "You know what makes this more difficult? I was beginning to care about her. I couldn't bring myself to tell Natalie that, but—"

"But she's your mother."

"She is. And she isn't that bad a person. The past few

weeks, since I've gotten to know her better, I almost…felt something for her.'' Abbie unconsciously worried the strap on her purse. ''It's hard to have someone come into my life, to care about them, and then, without much of a reason, they disappear. People have a way of leaving me behind.''

They rode on for a few moments of silence.

''Abbie?'' Jack's voice was soft, hesitant. ''This isn't the best time, and I know that, but something's come up.'' She inclined her head, irrationally thinking about the dirt and gravel on his floor mats. She'd warned him; this car was not made for South Dakota. ''Doc Winston likes the job I've been doing. Says I fit right in.''

''Oh? Really? That's good.''

''He's asked me to take over his practice, Abbie.'' Her heart started thudding, beating as irrationally as her thoughts. She turned on the seat, facing him. ''I have to make a decision soon. I've been thinking about it. A lot. There's no way to combine the best of both worlds because Cooper and Omaha are worlds apart. And, as for you and me, our private lives will tangle up our professional ones. Everything looks like a compromise.''

Oh, God. He's letting me down. Now. At the worst, most awful time of my life.

Be strong, she told herself, be strong and put on a good face and accept it.

''But sometimes, things like this force you to make a conscious choice,'' he went on, oblivious to her agony. ''And it works out. And makes you happier than you ever thought possible. Without all those tough, mind-boggling commitments.''

Okay, so she was wrong. Dead wrong.

He wanted a full-blown affair without any promises.

Forget it. Impossible. She couldn't do it.

Hours ago, she thought she, too, could take what she needed to sustain her and keep walking. But not anymore. The parameters, since her mother's disappearance, had changed. If she settled for that, she'd set herself up for heartbreak so big, so deep and wide, she'd never recover. "What do you want?" she asked, beating back the quaver in her voice.

"I hoped you'd help me figure that out."

"I'm afraid I'm not noble enough, or generous enough, to put your best interests first," she said. "My feelings would keep entering in."

"I don't see that as a hindrance," he said, his hand dropping so his thumb could stroke the fine bones of her wrist.

Tearing her gaze from their joined hands, she looked up in time to see the spot in which her mother's car had purportedly been found.

"There it is." Jack pointed to the dusty, dun-colored body that lay overturned in a dry, shallow creek bed.

"Omigod. Stop."

He pulled over, and she got out, shading her eyes to see down the slope. The wind was surprisingly warm on her face, and the sunshine on her shoulders like a massage. Tire tracks stretched for a thirty-yard skid before careening off the blacktop. From there, the weeds along the roadside were matted, the earth gouged. The sedan must have rolled at least three times. The car was balanced on its roof, looking like the victim of a battering ram. One lone strip of crumpled side molding snaked through the grass.

It was strange not to feel anything. But she didn't. Her mind was blank.

Jack moved to the other side of the car, her side, to stand next to her at the passenger door. He slung his arm around her shoulders and she, in turn, wrapped her arms around his middle.

"I wonder what happened," she said.

He shook his head.

Minutes passed as his palm chafed the muscles in her shoulders, the back of her neck.

Neither of them made a move to go closer to the accident site; they only stared at it.

"Jack," she said finally, "I want you to know that I love you dearly, but when you decide whether or not you should stay in Cooper, leave me out of it. It has to come down to what you want."

"In the past, my job's always come first—"

"I know that."

"But that doesn't mean—"

"Jack?" She leaned forward, shielding her eyes again. "What's that strange...that...?"

There was movement on the horizon. A spot of color that danced and dropped along the northwest ridge.

Danced?

No. Stumbled.

"Come on," he said, jerking on her arm.

They tore side by side over the uneven ground and through knee-high weeds. They ran a quarter of a mile before slipping through a barbed-wire fence separating them from the flailing figure in the adjoining pasture.

"It's her," Abbie panted, trying to keep pace with Jack's long strides.

They stopped short. The spectacle greeting them was disturbing, horrible. Abbie's mother, wearing only one shoe, groveled on the ground, her clothes torn and dirty. Blood, from a gash near her temple, matted her hair. After trickling down her cheek, it smudged over her mouth and chin. It was beet red, dried and crusty.

"Help me, help me," she cried, clawing at the hard-packed soil. Her bloodied fingers flexed brokenly.

Jack put his arm in front of Abbie to prevent her from rushing in. "Sylvie? We're here now."

"I have to get home," she wailed.

"I know. But I think you're hurt." He knelt beside her cautiously, his hands expertly exploring her wounds. Her

swollen forearms, the cuts and scrapes. He tilted her head
to peer into her dilated eyes.

"I have to get home," she pleaded. "My girls are waiting for me."

"It's okay," he soothed.

"I left them behind."

"Mama?"

"They miss me."

Abbie burst out crying, tears flowing unchecked down
her cheeks. "Mother, it's okay," she comforted, realizing
that, for the first time in decades, she truly meant it.

"They'll never forgive me."

"She's disoriented, Abbie."

Abbie nodded, unable to say anything.

"No broken bones. Probably dehydrated."

"This is Abbie, Mother."

"Abbie?"

"Yes."

"We have years to make up for."

"I know, Mother," she whispered brokenly. "We do."

At the hospital, Bob Worth smiled at Jack across his
wife's bed. Sylvie's hand was firmly entrenched in his, and
he looked like he was never going to let go. "Thank God
for cell phones."

Jack snorted, the noise very unprofessional for the white
lab coat he was wearing. "Abbie calls it the complementary
toy that goes with the convertible. It comes in handy. Particularly for emergency care."

"It wasn't just any care," Sylvie said. "It was you. I
remember. Bits and pieces of just about everything." She
ventured a tentative glance at Abbie, who stood at the end
of the bed with Natalie. She had just gotten off the phone
with Meredith, assuring her everything was all right.

"Traumatic head injuries have a way of doing that,"
Jack said. "I see it as a temporary memory loss, nothing

more. The bruises will go away, the cuts will heal. No internal injuries. We'll get a little more fluids into you and you'll be fine.''

Bob Worth grinned, his relieved features trembling with emotion. ''Couldn't stand to lose this girl again,'' he joked feebly, his eyes going misty as he stroked his wife's graying hair.

''Excuse me,'' Abbie mumbled as she turned away from the footboard of the bed. She had to leave the room. She couldn't bear to witness the love ebbing and flowing between her parents. It was too, too much.

The past twenty-four hours had been filled with chaos and confrontation. The police believed that her mother, disoriented from the accident, had wandered aimlessly into the grasslands, searching for help. She was lucky, they said. Lucky the temperatures were unseasonably warm, lucky she hadn't sustained permanent injuries.

Abbie trudged down to the end of the hall, wearily jamming her shoulder against the wall and gazing at the gum that someone had spit into the stainless-steel drain of the water fountain.

She'd always hated hospitals, visualizing tragedy or a pitiful story behind every door. Seeing Jack at work had changed some of that. The man was in his element. She could only imagine the confidence he must exude in the ER. How long would he really be content as a country doctor?

A hand was at her back, familiar in its warmth. ''Abbie? Hey, you okay?''

''Yeah.'' She pushed herself away from the wall. ''I...'' She broke off. ''Fine.''

''You're looking kind of skittish. What? You don't like my bedside manner?''

She smiled in spite of all the crazy emotions flooding her veins. ''I *love* your bedside manner,'' she confessed.

Jack chuckled, his wonderful dimples gracing the lines

of his face. "You know, someday we might get to finish what we started after the dance."

"I don't know. Real life keeps crowding in on us."

"Great. Then it'll remind us this isn't a fantasy." His elbow landed on the wall in front of her, eye level, encompassing her. "You survived the trauma team. You going into aftershock?"

"Excuse me?"

"Why'd you cut out, Abbie? Something I said?"

"No." She shook her head. "It's them. My folks. How do they do it, Jack? How do they manage it? A love that has sustained everything. Every trauma, every obstacle. Decades of absence and adversity. She's lying in a hospital bed, and they end up mooning over each other like teenagers. I envy them." Her lower lip quivered. "I'm sorry. I can't help it. Even with all the pain, I envy them. And I want the same. I don't think I could ever settle for less."

"You could have the same," he said. "With me."

Abbie's lower jaw slid off center.

"I want you to be my wife. I told Doc Winston I'm taking him up on his offer because I need to be here, near you. And Gramps's house. We put our hearts into it. We need to be the family who loves it."

"But—"

"Abigail Elizabeth Worth, I have never known a woman as strong, as resilient or as compassionate as you." She instinctively started objecting to the praise, but he waved her into silence. "I know, I know. You want your independence and this business thing, but I swear I'm going to build a life with you. If you want some time, I'll give you time. If you want to be wooed, I'll woo you. If—"

"No, Jack." Her hand fluttered to his chest, stopping him. "I want to be loved."

A heartbeat of yearning blipped away.

"I can do that," he offered quietly.

She stared up at him, wondering if he could do it or feel it. There was a decided difference.

"I love you, Abigail. With you, I want it all. The big wedding, with both families. You in a white dress, me in a tux. Rose petals on the white carpet—before they're on the pillowcases."

Her cheeks flushed. "I didn't think you knew."

He gave her his sexy, Brad Pitt grin. Then he leaned over and kissed her. Red-hot surges of passion, of desire, made her arms heavy, her legs weak.

"Mmm, yes," she mumbled against his mouth.

Behind him, someone uncomfortably cleared her throat. "Doctor?"

"Mmm. Yes?" he said, lifting an eyebrow as he dragged his mouth away.

"I think you're needed at the end of the hall. There seems to be some commotion. With your new patient."

Jack looked over Abbie's shoulder. Abbie turned.

The three of them, Bob, Natalie and Sylvie, with her IV still attached, peered out the doorway of her room.

"Well, you did it, didn't you, Jack Conroy?" Natalie crowed.

"Did what?" Jack said, moving away as he settled Abbie more closely inside the circle of his arm.

"You just popped the question!"

Abbie's stride faltered. "How'd she know that?" she demanded in a whisper as she gave Jack a sideways look.

"She's your sister. I haven't a clue."

They kept walking.

Abbie zeroed in on Natalie. "And for your information, bigmouth, I just said yes."

"You did?" Jack said, surprised.

"I did. Mmm, yes," she repeated. "But Nat had to go and—"

"Girls, girls," her father intoned.

"Natalie. Let her break the news," her mother chided

before smiling fondly at Jack, then Abbie. To her husband, she said, "He's such a nice young man, isn't he, Robert?"

"He is."

"And he's going to be in the family. There'll probably be grandchildren."

"More'n likely."

"Omaha isn't *that* far," her mother went on.

"Wait a minute," Abbie intervened before her parents had her life planned for her. "We aren't going to Omaha. Jack's taking over Doc Winston's practice."

"And Gramps's place seems to suit us," Jack said, "so we want to call that home."

"Oh, boy!" her mother exclaimed. "And it's just down the road!"

"Smart boy," her father said, nodding approvingly.

Abbie and Jack exchanged contented smiles.

Natalie only laughed. "Attaboy, Jack," she quipped. "I'm proud of you. You couldn't do any better than my sister."

* * * * *

SOMETIMES THE SMALLEST PACKAGES CAN LEAD TO THE BIGGEST SURPRISES!

Bundles of JOY

February 1999
A VOW, A RING, A BABY SWING
by Teresa Southwick (SR #1349)

Pregnant and alone, Rosie Marchetti had just been stood up at the altar. So family friend Steve Schafer stepped up the aisle and married her. Now Rosie is trying to convince him that this family was meant to be....

May 1999
THE BABY ARRANGEMENT
by Moyra Tarling (SR #1368)

Jared McAndrew has been searching for his son, and when he discovers Faith Nelson with his child he demands she come home with him. Can Faith convince Jared that he has the wrong mother—but the right bride?

Enjoy these stories of love and family. And look for future BUNDLES OF JOY titles from Leanna Wilson and Suzanne McMinn coming in the fall of 1999.

BUNDLES OF JOY
only from

⍟ *Silhouette*®

Available wherever Silhouette books are sold.

Coming in May 1999

BABY Fever

by
New York Times Bestselling Author

KASEY MICHAELS

When three sisters hear their biological
clocks ticking, they know it's
time for action.

But who will they get to father their babies?

**Find out how the road to motherhood
leads to love in this brand-new collection.**

Available at your favorite retail outlet.

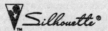

Silhouette®

Silhouette
ROMANCE™

COMING NEXT MONTH

#1372 I MARRIED THE BOSS!—Laura Anthony
Loving the Boss

Sophia Shepherd wanted to marry the ideal man, and her new boss, Rex Michael Barrington III, was as dreamy as they came! But when an overheard conversation had him testing her feelings, Sophia had to prove she wanted more than just a dream....

#1373 HIS TEN-YEAR-OLD SECRET—Donna Clayton
Fabulous Fathers

Ten years of longing were over. Tess Galloway had returned to claim the child she'd thought lost to her forever. But Dylan Minster, her daughter's father and the only man she'd ever loved, would not let Tess have her way without a fight, and without her heart!

#1374 THE RANCHER AND THE HEIRESS—Susan Meier
Texas Family Ties

City girl Alexis MacFarland wasn't thrilled about spending a year on a ranch—even if it meant she'd inherit half of it! But one look at ranch owner Caleb Wright proved it wouldn't be *that* bad, *if* she could convince him she'd be his cowgirl for good.

#1375 THE MARRIAGE STAMPEDE—Julianna Morris
Wranglers & Lace

Wrangler Merrie Foster and stockbroker Logan Kincaid were *nothing* alike. She wanted kids and country life, and he wanted wealth and the city. But when they ended up in a mock engagement, would the sparks between them overcome their differences?

#1376 A BRIDE IN WAITING—Sally Carleen
On the Way to a Wedding

Stand in for a missing bride? Sara Martin didn't mind, especially as a favor for Dr. Lucas Daniels. But when her life became filled with wedding plans and stolen kisses, Sara knew she wanted to change from stand-in bride to wife forever!

#1377 HUSBAND FOUND—Martha Shields
Family Matters

Single mother Emma Lockwood needed a job...and R. D. Johnson was offering one. Trouble was, Rafe was Emma's long-lost husband—and he didn't recognize her! Could she help him recover his memory—and the love they once shared?